MARKED FOR DEATH

Driskoll ran into the tiny guardhouse. Kellach was staring at something stuck in the wall.

"It came right through the door," Kellach said, pointing at the shiny object. "Someone threw it at me. But I moved and it missed."

Driskoll looked at the shining silver handle of a dagger. It was carved with the emblem of the Knights of the Silver Dragon.

Kellach reached up and slowly pried it out of the wall. He held it up and stared at it.

Driskoll could see the familiar but strange runes on the guard, and his own stunned expression staring back at him from the mirror-like blade.

And he could see the seven letters burned into it: KELLACH.

DAGGER of DOOM

KERRY DANIEL ROBERTS

BOOK 6

COVER & INTERIOR ART
EMILY FIEGENSHUH

MIRROR
STONE

Dagger of Doom

©2005 Wizards of the Coast, Inc.

Distributed in the United States by Holtzbrinck Publishing. Distributed in Canada by Fenn Ltd.

Distributed to the hobby, toy, and comic trade in the United States and Canada by regional distributors.

Distributed worldwide by Wizards of the Coast, Inc. and regional distributors.

Printed in the U.S.A.

Cover and interior art by Emily Fiegenschuh
Cartography by Dennis Kauth
First Printing: April 2005
Library of Congress Catalog Card Number: 2004114593

9 8 7 6 5 4 3 2 1

US ISBN: 0-7869-3631-2
ISBN-13: 978-0-7869-3631-1
620-17723000-001-EN

U.S., CANADA,
ASIA, PACIFIC, & LATIN AMERICA
Wizards of the Coast, Inc.
P.O. Box 707
Renton, WA 98057-0707
+1-800-324-6496

EUROPEAN HEADQUARTERS
Wizards of the Coast, Belgium
T Hofveld 6d
1702 Groot-Bijgaarden
Belgium
+322 457 3350

Visit our website at **www.mirrorstonebooks.com**

For Katie, the fairest, truest, kindest knight I ever met

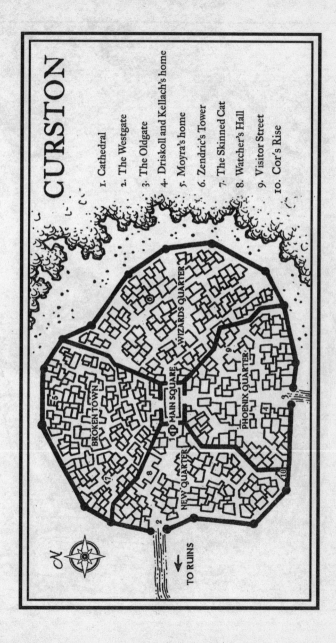

CURSTON

1. Cathedral
2. The Westgate
3. The Oldgate
4. Driskoll and Kellach's home
5. Moyra's home
6. Zendric's Tower
7. The Skinned Cat
8. Watcher's Hall
9. Visitor Street
10. Cor's Rise

BROKEN TOWN

WIZARDS QUARTER

MAIN SQUARE

NEW QUARTER

PHOENIX QUARTER

TO RUINS

CHAPTER

I

"Stop reading!"

Driskoll dropped the scroll onto the dusty ground.

He looked up and saw two tiny eyes squinting at him from behind blubbery yellow cheeks. Oswald stood over Driskoll, nibbling a block of cheese. His dirty white robes stretched tight across his stomach, making the old bard look like a fat gray rat.

Oswald's scowling face turned a shade darker. It was almost the same color as the orange cheese in his hand.

"Pick up that scroll! How many times must I tell you?" Oswald shouted, spitting a blob of chewed cheese onto Driskoll's nose. "Parchment is expensive. You must take care of it."

Driskoll flicked the chewed-up cheese gob off his nose. "Sorry, Oswald. It won't happen again."

"You're right it won't. If you spent less time reading scrolls and more time erasing them, you wouldn't be making such stupid mistakes."

Driskoll blinked at the old bard. "I was only looking—"

Bits of cheese flew out of Oswald's mouth in a blizzard of orange fury. "Insolence! Disrespect!" he sputtered. "Why did I let your father talk me into hiring you to be a scrolltender, even if it was just for a month?"

Oswald clasped his chest. "You will kill me before the summer is over!"

Driskoll rolled his eyes. The writing on the parchment wasn't very interesting anyway. Maybe he could find another one and bring it home to look at that night.

"And don't get any ideas about bringing scrolls home to read." Oswald jabbed a pudgy finger in Driskoll's back. "I'll know if any are missing." The old bard then whirled around and stomped back inside his house.

Driskoll's shoulders slumped. He turned back to the large black cauldron in the center of Oswald's garden.

The water was already boiling. He scooped out a handful of purifying crystals from the bucket nearby and dumped them in the water. The mixture began sizzling and popping ferociously. Miniature waves thrashed, their tips foaming white like thousands of sharp teeth.

Driskoll picked the scroll he had been reading off the ground and dangled it over the furious potion.

"Please don't throw me in, Mister Bard," Driskoll squealed in a tiny voice that sounded a lot like Oswald's. "The potion—it will kill me before the summer is over."

He held it high. "No, no!" he squeaked, dropping it into the cauldron. "Aaaugh!" The helpless ink drifted off the page and into the madly swirling potion. Driskoll watched as the potion devoured the ink, leaving the parchment behind.

He laughed. When you worked for Old Oswald as a scroll tender, you had to make your own entertainment.

"I hear that laughing!" Oswald called from the doorway. "Scroll tenders do not laugh! Now, stop dawdling and get to work!"

Driskoll sighed.

"Here's another one for you." Oswald tossed a roll of parchment through the open door. Driskoll barely managed to catch it.

"That one came from the ruins," Oswald snapped, "so be sure you add more purifying crystals. You never know what kind of evil magic is in there."

As Driskoll gripped the scroll, he felt the irresistible urge to read it. It was almost as if the ancient paper were calling to him, whispering: O*pen me. Read me.*

"And for the last time! Don't read the scrolls!" And with that, Oswald slammed the door shut, making the whole back wall of his house tremble.

Of course, telling Driskoll not to read the scroll made him want to do exactly the opposite. Gripping the tightly rolled paper, he crept around to the other side of the cauldron, making sure to avoid the sparks from the fire underneath the pot.

He took a quick glance around the cauldron. Good. The door was still shut.

Flopping back onto the ground, he settled into a comfortable reading position. Slowly, he unrolled the parchment.

What he saw nearly made him fall into the flames.

There, on the browning, aged paper was a charcoal drawing of a dagger. The sketch was vivid in every detail. The dagger's

3

broad blade almost seemed to poke up off the page. A Knights of the Silver Dragon emblem was emblazoned on the dagger's hilt. And beneath the drawing, in looping cursive writing was a caption that read: The Dagger of Doom.

But that wasn't what had so frightened Driskoll.

What frightened Driskoll was the name etched on the blade: KELLACH.

CHAPTER

2

D riskoll stared at the drawing. It wasn't every day that he came across a picture of a dagger with his own brother's name carved into it.

Driskoll tore his eyes away from the drawing and peeked around the side of the cauldron. Through the window, he could see the bard hunched over his scrolls.

Oswald looked up and rapped on the window. Driskoll could hear his muffled cry through the glass panes. "What are you doing out there? Get that scroll in the potion."

Driskoll ducked back behind the cauldron. He took one last look at the drawing.

He heard the click of the door opening. Now he was in trouble. He had sat behind the cauldron for too long and Oswald was suspicious.

But this scroll was too important to be erased in the potion. Kellach would want to see it.

Suddenly, Driskoll had an idea. He reached inside his jacket pocket. His hand felt a small bag of chocolates he'd bought earlier that morning. No, not that. He dug deeper into his pocket. There!

He gripped an old scroll he'd found at home in the storage closet weeks earlier. It was pretty dull stuff—some old business document that showed the prices of pigs a hundred years ago. Driskoll had known it would come in handy for something, and this was his chance. He pulled out the old scroll.

He could hear the back door swinging open and the sound of Oswald's panting as the bard waddled toward him.

Still hidden behind the cauldron, Driskoll quickly rolled up the dagger drawing and tucked it inside his pocket.

"Eh, boy! What are you doing?"

With the drawing hidden safely inside his pocket, Driskoll popped up. He dumped the business scroll into the cauldron, pigs and all.

The old bard reached the cauldron just as the parchment began its helpless swirl around in the potion.

Oswald gave Driskoll a suspicious look and peered in the black pot.

Had Oswald seen him exchanging the scrolls? Driskoll looked into the cauldron. He half expected to see words spelling out "check his pocket" in the potion. But all he could see was parchment and inky black bubbles.

Ffffllpppt. The cauldron belched a column of white steam into the old bard's face.

Oswald coughed and staggered a little.

Driskoll relaxed his shoulders. White steam was a good sign. Black or red steam would have meant that dangerous black magic lurked inside those scrolls. And that would mean extra work for Driskoll.

Or worse. A cursed scroll could change his skin to blue or turn his ears into tomatoes. It happened all the time, and Driskoll was getting used to it.

The old bard wiped his face as Driskoll stirred the cauldron with an innocent smile on his face.

Oswald muttered and hobbled back to the house.

Driskoll grabbed a pair of tongs and carefully lifted a piece of soggy parchment from the potion.

He laid the sheet out in the sun to dry. A few hours and it would be almost as good as new parchment.

As he leaned over, the scroll in his pocket poked into his side.

A twinge of guilt shot through Driskoll. "I'm just borrowing the scroll," he insisted to himself. "I'll return it . . . as soon as I find out what it means."

■ ■ ▮ ■ ▮

"You erased all of them?" The bard took a bite of cheese and looked down at Driskoll from his high stool.

"Yes," Driskoll said wearily, dumping the stack of clean and dried parchment on a table next to the bard's high desk.

"Let me see your arms."

Driskoll held out his arms.

"Hmmm." The bard tapped his many chins. "No green skin, no oozing sores. I was sure that scroll from the ruins . . ."

He turned and began rifling through a stack of rolled parchment on his desk.

Driskoll couldn't stop thinking about the scroll in his pocket. He had to know more about it. Be direct, he told himself. Just ask.

"What's the Dagger of Doom?" Driskoll asked.

Scrolls shot into the air as the bard grasped his chest. "You looked at it! How many times must I tell you to keep your nosy eyes off the scrolls? Oh, you shall be the death of me. I shall tell your father. He will know how to deal with you—"

"But that dagger had my brother's name on it."

"What utter nonsense! It had no such thing. I looked at it myself. It's that ridiculous legend again."

"What legend?" Driskoll asked.

The bard stuffed another bite of cheese into his mouth and accidentally bit his finger. "Ouch! It is none of your business. It is your business to clean scrolls so that they can be used again."

Oswald pulled an odd-looking green scroll off his desk and handed it to Driskoll. "Now, if you ever wish to become a great bard—like myself—you will go now and scrub that green scroll. Hard."

Driskoll sighed. "Great bard," he mumbled under his breath. "I can tell stories far better than you ever could . . . "

"What did you say?"

"Nothing." Driskoll picked at the seal on the strange green scroll. Maybe the direct approach wasn't the best way to get information.

"And bring me a bandage for my finger," Oswald said. "And some bread."

Driskoll wondered how the old bard got anything done when all he did was eat. It gave him another idea. He put down the green scroll and reached into his jacket pocket. There was the dagger scroll he'd hidden earlier. And there was the small wax bag of chocolates.

8

Driskoll drew the bag out of his pocket. The bard sniffed and looked down at him.

Driskoll opened the bag and removed a small, thick square of chocolate fudge. He'd been saving it for later, but this was important. He held it up to Oswald.

"Eh boy, what have you got there?" Oswald asked.

Driskoll took a bite. "Mmm," he said. "Fresh chocolate."

The bard licked his lips.

Driskoll swallowed loudly. "I guess I'll clean that scroll now."

"Eh, one moment, boy." The bard eased off his stool and reached for the bag. "Is there any more of that?"

"Oh sorry." Driskoll held the bag away. "I got it at the market this morning and it was the last batch." He licked his finger. "But you should really try it sometime."

A small pool of saliva formed at the corner of the bard's thin lips. "Eh, perhaps you could share?"

"You know, I would like to," Driskoll said. "But I really wanted to know about that dagger." Driskoll took out another piece of fudge and popped it in his mouth. "Melts in your mouth."

"All right, all right. Give me the chocolate and I will tell you."

"No." Driskoll smiled. "You tell the story first. Then you get the chocolate."

Oswald kept his eyes on the bag of chocolates as Driskoll sat down to listen. Getting the bard to talk was easier than he would have thought. Driskoll would have to remember this tactic.

Oswald reached for the tankard on his desk and took a large gulp. Then he breathed deeply and shut his eyes.

For a moment Driskoll thought Oswald had fallen asleep, but the bard opened his eyes and began speaking as if he were in a trance.

"Long ago, two brothers lived here in Curston, back when it was still known as Promise. They lived in a place called Promise Castle. The boys' names were Cor and Adrian.

"Cor was a wizard and a Knight of the Silver Dragon. He was admired for his bravery. But mostly, he was known for protecting a race of magical creatures known as mantlehorn.

"Adrian was a wizard and an artisan. He was known for his stonecutting and glasswork and also for his fantastical inventions. But unlike his brother, he was not chosen to be a knight.

"Every time Cor went out to battle, Adrian was left behind. He grew angry and bitter at being left out. The brothers argued often.

"Cor, who was a good and just knight, felt sorry for his brother. So one day Cor presented Adrian with a unique weapon: a mirrored dagger. Cor had received it as a gift for protecting the mantlehorn, but he thought that the dagger, which could cut through stone easily and swiftly, would serve Adrian in his mason work.

"But Adrian saw the dagger as an insult and another sign that his brother lorded his knighthood over him. He became furious with Cor and flew into a rage. He took the dagger and plunged it into his brother's heart. He ran off and was never heard from again.

"When they pulled the weapon from Cor's chest, Cor's name was emblazoned on the blade. The mantlehorn carried Cor away and buried him with the dagger.

"That is why it is known to this day as the Dagger of Doom. It is said that the mantlehorn shall return with the dagger someday, bringing it to brothers who cannot reconcile. And the brother whose name appears on the blade is marked for death."

The bard seemed to come out of his trance. He snatched the bag of chocolates from Driskoll's hands. But Driskoll barely noticed.

"My brother's name was on that dagger drawing," he said.

"What?" The bard shouted through a mouthful of chocolate. "Are you still telling lies? If anyone's name should be on there, it should be mine. Considering how much I suffer because of you, death would be a relief."

"But I saw Kellach's name on there."

"You saw no such thing," the bard said, huddled over the bag of chocolates. "And anyway, it does not matter. You erased the scroll. The drawing is gone." He looked up. "You did erase it, didn't you?"

Driskoll took a step back.

"Yes," he said. "I erased all the scrolls."

It wasn't really a lie—he did erase the scrolls. Driskoll bent down to pick up the green scroll. He would clean it the next day. Right now, he needed to talk to Kellach.

But his head suddenly felt itchy.

The bard looked down at Driskoll. His chocolate-smeared mouth broke into a gleeful smile. "Ahh, now that's more like it."

II

Driskoll headed for the door. "I'm off," he said, scratching his head. "It's almost curfew."

"Very good," the bard said with a giggle. "And thank you, young bard, for the entertainment."

CHAPTER

3

Driskoll had no idea what Oswald was talking about, but he ran straight home. He tore through the door and found Kellach sitting in the front room, studying his spellbook.

As Driskoll stomped into the room, Kellach looked up and smirked. "Bad day at the bard's?"

"I have something to show you," Driskoll panted as something green crawled down his nose. He swiped it away as he reached into his pocket and pulled out the scroll. He held it up to Kellach.

Kellach leaned back and pointed at Driskoll's head. "Did this scroll do that to you?"

"What?"

Kellach pointed at a mirror hanging over the fireplace.

Driskoll turned and jumped when he saw his reflection.

His hair had turned green. And it was moving.

"Oh great. I knew there was something strange about that green scroll. It was cursed!"

Kellach stood behind him. "Caterpillars. It turned your hair into fuzzy little caterpillars." He snickered.

Driskoll turned away from the mirror. "Can you just do a spell and get rid of them, Kellach? This is important."

"Sure." Kellach grinned. "But I'll have to send them all the way through their metamorphosis before I can get your hair back."

"Whatever," Driskoll said, pulling a wriggling caterpillar out of his eyebrow. "Just do it quickly. I've got to show you this."

Still snickering, Kellach raised his arms and mumbled something at Driskoll's head. Driskoll felt a tightening, as if the skin on his skull were being pulled in every direction. This didn't feel like his normal hair. Something was wrong. He looked in the mirror. His head was covered in tiny, white cottony pieces of fluff.

Kellach roared with laughter. "Nice hairdo!"

Driskoll tapped his foot. "Hurry up! How am I supposed to do anything with a head full of cocoons?"

Kellach slapped his knee. "I guess you'll just have to—wing it." He burst into more guffaws.

Driskoll groaned. "Will you just please undo the curse?"

"I'm trying." Kellach doubled over and held his stomach. "But I can't lift curses when I'm laughing."

When Kellach was finally able to straighten up, he mumbled something again. Driskoll could hear soft fluttering, and his head tickled. He looked up. Thousands of tiny orange wings flapped around his head.

"Kellach!"

But Kellach was lying on the floor. His mouth was open and nothing was coming out. Every time he tried to stand and look

14

at Driskoll, he burst into choking guffaws and went down on his knees again.

It took ten minutes for Kellach to finally finish the spell without snickering.

"I'm glad I could provide so much entertainment," Driskoll said in a dignified voice as he smoothed his hair.

"Don't you want to be a bard? That's what they do." Kellach wiped the tears from his eyes.

"You're a wizard's apprentice! You're not supposed to laugh at people when you're doing spells."

Kellach shrugged.

"Ah, forget it," Driskoll said. "This is more important anyway. You need to see this." Driskoll opened the scroll.

"No thanks, I like my head the way it is." Kellach took a step back.

"This scroll didn't curse me. It was another one," Driskoll said impatiently, pointing at the drawing. "Look at the drawing, Kellach. Have you ever seen this before?"

Kellach glanced at it, still at a safe distance. "Nope."

"It's a picture of the Dagger of Doom. It's supposed to appear to brothers who can't reconcile, and the person whose name appears on it is marked for death."

"Very funny, Dris," Kellach said disinterestedly. "But you'll have to do better than that."

"No, this isn't a joke. Look!" Driskoll tapped the parchment. "Your name is on it, Kellach! You're marked for death."

"Nice try. How long did it take you to draw that?" Kellach said, peering at the drawing. "You might want to redo the hilt there. The perspective looks a bit off."

"Listen to me, Kellach!" Driskoll stomped his foot. "I didn't draw this! I found it. It's some sort of magical dagger. There were two brothers. And one of them killed the other one."

"Uh-huh." Kellach was walking around the room, picking up books that had been thrown on the floor. "Where's that blasted spellbook?"

Driskoll followed him around the room. "One of the brothers, Cor, died when his name appeared on the dagger," he explained. "And I think you're in trouble now too. The scroll is a warning."

Click.

"What was that?" Kellach asked, stopping suddenly.

"I don't know. It sounded like the window opening in the kitchen," Driskoll said. "Is Dad home?"

"No, he's working tonight," Kellach answered.

Click.

"There it is again."

"I think someone just unlocked the kitchen window," Kellach whispered.

Driskoll drew his sword as the brothers crept silently toward the kitchen. Kellach threw open the door.

"Who's there?" he shouted. The kitchen window was open, and a shadowy figure stood before them. The figure raised an arm.

"I'm a wizard," Kellach said a little breathlessly. "I can dissolve you in fire."

"Fire?" A familiar voice muttered. "Demon dung, Kellach. You can do better than that." The figure lit a torch and held it up. Driskoll could see a shock of red hair.

"Hey orc brains, it's me." Moyra grinned at them in the torchlight.

Driskoll and Kellach didn't move.

"Well don't just stand there staring like a couple of bugbears," she said, pulling up a wooden chair.

"How did you get that window open?" Kellach said, lowering his arms.

Moyra shrugged. "You know I can break into anything." She was checking out a basket of fruit on the table. "But you really need to put in better locks. I mean, come on, it took me thirty seconds to get in here."

"Why couldn't you just knock on the front door, like normal people?" Driskoll asked.

"I'm not like normal people." She reached for an apple. "I saw you running home, Dris. I called you, but you didn't answer. What happened to your hair?"

Driskoll touched his head to make sure everything was still there, but he didn't answer.

"Whatcha got there?" She pointed at the scroll.

Driskoll showed her the scroll and explained the legend of the Dagger of Doom while Kellach made a lot of impatient noises. Moyra stared at Driskoll for a few seconds after he had finished the story.

"What's a mantlehorn?" she asked finally.

"I don't know," Driskoll answered. "But that's not nearly as important as what I saw on this drawing." He pointed at the scroll. "Kellach's name is on the dagger."

Moyra took another apple and bit into it. She studied the drawing. "So where did this scroll come from?"

Kellach chuckled. "It came from Driskoll's imagination. He just made this whole story up to scare me."

Driskoll gave his brother a sharp glare and turned back to Moyra. "I did *not* make this up! Moyra, you've got to believe me. Oswald said the scroll came from the ruins—"

"The ruins?" Moyra interrupted. "Did you send it through that purifying potion of yours yet?"

"Why would I do that?" Driskoll answered. "That would erase the drawing."

Moyra got up and thrust her face toward Driskoll. "Because it's from the *roo-ins*." She said it slowly and carefully, as if he were three years old. "It's probably cursed! That's probably why it had Kellach's name on it. And I bet those mantleworts are monsters from the ruins. When they come back with the dagger, they're not just going to walk up to you and say, 'Oh hi, here's a pretty dagger for you.' They're going to kill you with it."

Driskoll rolled his eyes. "They're mantlehorn, not mantleworts. And that's what I've been trying to tell you. The dagger is dangerous. This scroll is a warning."

Moyra looked at Kellach. "Do you know what it means?"

Kellach scoffed. "It means the caterpillars got inside Driskoll's brain," he said, grabbing a cloak and turning to the door.

"Where are you going?" Driskoll asked.

"None of your business," Kellach said.

"But you can't go out. It's after curfew. And anyway, haven't you been listening to me? Someone is going to try to kill you with that dagger. You're in danger."

Kellach snorted. "The only person who's in danger around here is you if you don't get rid of that scroll. Don't wait up for me." He opened the kitchen door. "And don't forget Zendric's harpy. It's your turn to feed her tomorrow morning." He tossed a golden key at Driskoll and then disappeared, slamming the door behind him.

Moyra took a last bite of apple. "What's with him?"

"Dunno. Probably feeling all alone since Zendric left yesterday."

"Where'd he go?" Moyra asked.

Driskoll shrugged. "Vacation."

"Vacation?" Moyra looked surprised for the first time that evening. "Zendric doesn't go on vacations."

"Well, he did. Wouldn't you want a vacation if Kellach were your apprentice?"

CHAPTER

4

Driskoll awoke late the next morning. After Moyra had gone home, Driskoll had stayed up waiting for Kellach, but he fell asleep before Kellach made it home.

He sat up and looked in Kellach's bed. It was already made. He could hear someone banging around in the kitchen. Maybe Kellach was making breakfast. He got dressed and went downstairs.

A tall, dark-haired man wearing the uniform of the captain of the watch sat at the table eating bread and jam. He was jotting some notes on a piece of parchment and didn't look up when Driskoll came in.

"Hi, Dad."

Torin smirked at his son. "Sleep late again?"

Driskoll yawned and looked hopefully at the bread in Torin's hands.

"Here," Torin said, handing it to him. "I'm not hungry anyway."

Driskoll accepted the bread and took a large bite.

"You would do well to get up earlier like your brother. He left before even I was awake," Torin said.

Driskoll looked hard at the bread in his hands. He hated being compared to Kellach. He was about to say something about Kellach going out after curfew the night before when Torin stood up.

"Stay out of trouble today," Torin warned. "We've had a lot of strangers coming into town, and I don't need any more headaches."

"What strangers?"

Torin drew on his coat. "Big construction job." He sighed. "Some kind of castle. It's a nightmare." He rubbed his temple with one hand. "Workers are coming in from all over. Strange types. We've had to put extra men at the gates to make sure no one slips in from the ruins."

"They're building a castle in Curston?"

"Yes," Torin said. "Although why we need one is beyond me." He looked at Driskoll. "It's in the Old Quarter, so keep out of there. Stay at Oswald's and do your work. A construction site is no place for kids."

"Dad, I'm a Knight of the Silver Dragon. I've been in more dangerous situations than some building thing. Remember last month when Kellach and I—"

"Just do your job at Oswald's," Torin said sternly. "You may be a Knight, but you're still twelve years old. You don't need any more danger."

Driskoll frowned. Torin reached out awkwardly and clapped his hand on Driskoll's back. But he smacked his son harder than he meant to, and it knocked Driskoll forward a little.

They both chuckled uncomfortably and looked around the room.

"Well," Torin said. "I, uh, should be going. Bye."

He swept out the door leaving Driskoll alone with his thoughts.

A castle in Curston? Castles usually meant kings and queens, but Curston didn't have anything like that. Who would be building a castle?

He wondered why Oswald hadn't said something about it. I bet Zendric told Kellach about it before he went away, he thought.

Zendric told Kellach all kinds of interesting things in the course of teaching him wizardry.

All I get are caterpillars in my hair, Driskoll thought.

He finished his bread and left the house. His first stop was the butcher's tent.

"Don't tell me," the butcher said when Driskoll arrived. "You need some rotting meat."

"How'd you know?" Driskoll asked.

"Your brother was here yesterday looking for the same thing. And Zendric last week. I don't know what that old wizard is thinking by keeping a harpy as a pet."

"Wish I could tell you." Driskoll sighed. "He found her last week, injured. Said having a harpy that owes him her life would be a handy thing to have around."

"Handy?" The butcher laughed as he reached into a bucket. "Well, at least I'm getting rid of meat I can't sell."

Driskoll scrunched up his nose as the butcher pulled out a lump of stringy, brownish meat clinging to a massive bone.

"Here," he said. "This is from yesterday."

Driskoll took a step back.

"Go ahead," the butcher said. "It's not going to eat *you*."

Driskoll didn't like to hear the word "eat" associated with the piece of rotting flesh in front of him. But he took it and hurried to Zendric's. The sooner he could be rid of the thing, the better.

He reached into his pocket and drew out the long golden key that Kellach had given him the night before. He put the key in the lock and clicked open the door.

"Kellach?"

No one answered.

Driskoll took a step inside and looked around the main room. The books were stacked neatly along the mantle of the fieldstone fireplace on one side of the room. Two fat armchairs sat in front of the hearth. Instructional tapestries, detailing spells and the lives of famous wizards, and star maps hung above the work desks near the back wall. Bookshelves filled with ancient tomes and odd magical implements lined the wall. The statue of Boudica, the warrior queen who had died in the Sundering of the Seal, stood in a far corner.

Everything looked normal, but the place was strangely silent.

"Kellach?" he called again at the base of the polished wood staircase that led up to the tower. There was no answer.

He climbed the stairs and came to the ironbound door leading to Zendric' private workroom.

He opened the door, and a smell hit him like a suffocating blanket. It was deathlike and moldy, and it drove thoughts of the missing Kellach straight from his mind. He held an arm up to his nose and mouth and took a step inside.

A large iron cage took up nearly half the room. Inside, in the far corner, lay a large, blood red, egg-shaped object. A sound like snoring was coming from it. As Driskoll took a few tentative steps toward the cage, the egg thing quivered and the snoring stopped. A small flap lifted at the top, revealing a flat, black eye.

Driskoll stepped forward. The eye followed him. Just as he reached the cage, the flap opened further, extending several feet in the air, into a large reptilian wing.

Another wing unfolded, and an ugly woman sprang up between them. Her matted black hair stood straight up out of her head, and she grimaced wildly at Driskoll like some kind of demon. She flexed the powerful muscles in her sinewy arms and opened and closed her clawlike fists.

Driskoll gulped. One squeeze of those claws around his neck and he could forget about the meat he was carrying—he'd be the main course.

But the birdlike black eyes honed in on the meat, and the harpy took some deep, wheezing breaths. Driskoll quickly dropped the bone between the bars. The harpy raced over and grabbed it in her big hands as Driskoll moved several feet away in about two seconds.

Driskoll looked away, wishing he could put the sound of her gnashing teeth out of his mind. He was just about to slip out when something croaked behind him.

"Bardman."

Driskoll stopped.

"Bardman tell story."

He turned and looked at the harpy. She was holding the meat with one hand, and grimacing at him.

"Ruida like stories. Bardman tell story."

Driskoll wasn't even aware that harpies could talk, let alone listen to stories. And how did she know he was a bard?

"Um," Driskoll said in a small voice, "I've got to go—"

Ruida hurled the meat on the floor and flew up against the side of the cage. "Story!" She banged on the bars with her fist. The cage shook violently, nearly toppling over. "Story!" she screamed, and her red wings flapped madly.

"Okay, okay," Driskoll said as calmly as he could, which was no mean feat, considering that he was shaking all over.

The harpy stopped screaming and walked calmly back to the meat. She picked up her bone. "Bardman tell story," she croaked.

Driskoll searched his mind desperately trying to think of a story. Nothing came. Finally, he remembered the Dagger of Doom.

She pointed with her elbow at a wooden stool, and Driskoll guessed she wanted him to sit in it. "Bardman stay. Tell story. Wizardboy not ever stay. Ruida not like Wizardboy. Too high and mighty."

Driskoll smirked. Wizardboy. Was she talking about Kellach?

"All right," he muttered. "You want a story? I'll tell you a story."

He settled uneasily on the stool and began to tell the story of the Dagger of Doom in a shaky voice.

It was very unnerving to tell a story while she crunched on

the bone, but by the time he was finished, he had at least stopped shaking.

"Good story," Ruida said.

"Okay." Driskoll stood up and headed for the door. "Now that you've, uh, eaten, I'll just be going—"

"Harpies steal dagger like one in story."

Driskoll put his hand on the doorknob. "That's nice." And then Ruida's words sunk in. His head whipped back to look at her. "Wait. What did you just say?"

"Harpies steal dagger."

"You stole a dagger? What did it look like?"

The harpy pointed a long, black fingernail at Driskoll. "Look like that."

"It looked like me?"

"No. That." She was pointing above the door. Driskoll looked up and saw a plaque bearing the Knights of the Silver Dragon seal hanging above the threshold.

"That's the Knights of the Silver Dragon seal. Zendric—I mean, Wizardman—is a Knight. And so am I."

"Yah, look like that. Give to Ruida so she can see better."

Driskoll stepped forward, then stopped. She'd have to get the seal over his dead body, which she was probably about to do anyway. He had a better idea.

He reached into his pocket and pulled out the scroll with the dagger drawing. Unrolling it carefully, he held it up and showed it to her. "Did it look like this?"

"Ruida old. Can't see nothing."

Driskoll brought the drawing closer to the cage. The smell nearly knocked him to his knees.

Ruida squinted at the drawing of the dagger.

"Yah," she said. "Dagger look just like that, Bardman."

Driskoll rolled up the scroll. "Where is the dagger now?"

The harpy looked around the cage. "Ruida not know. Harpies take dagger. Ruida old. Fly too slow. Get hit with arrow. Ruida hurt bad. Crash into Wizardman's tower. Wake up and dagger gone. Other harpies gone too. Wizardman give food."

"So what did you do with the dagger?" Driskoll asked.

"Ruida told you, Bardman. Not know nothing. Just take to city."

"You took it here? To Curston? Do you know where?"

"Ruida tell Bardman all she know." The harpy settled back into the corner of the cage, clutching her bone and taking deep, rattling breaths.

"Wait," she said. "Some harpies talk about castle. Maybe took dagger there."

"Castle? What castle?"

The harpy coughed loudly. It was a horrible, hacking cough.

"Ruida . . . still . . . hungry," she wheezed.

Driskoll stared at her.

"Bring more . . . or Ruida break out of cage . . . peck Bardman's eyes out."

Driskoll's mouth fell open. She said it as if it were something she did every day. The cage was made of iron, but she had shaken it before as if it were a tiny, wooden box.

"I'll find you some more meat," he promised. "I have to go right now, or I'll be late to my job. But I'll bring you some more later. Then maybe you can tell me more about the dagger."

"Good Bardman," she wheezed. "Bring Ruida more meat." She curled into her egg shape again and began snoring.

Driskoll raced down the stairs. He had never been so happy to go to Old Oswald's.

CHAPTER

5

Oswald chuckled as Driskoll ran into the bard's study. "I see your brother, the wizard, fixed you up."

Driskoll swept his hand through his hair as he remembered the curse and how Kellach had removed it. That reminded him.

Where was Kellach? A picture of the Dagger of Doom with Kellach's name on it flashed in his mind.

And the brother whose name appears on the blade is marked for death, Oswald had said.

He was about to ask Oswald to tell him more about the dagger, but a knock at the door interrupted him.

He went to the heavy oak door and opened it. A tall figure dressed in a brown cloak stood framed in the doorway. Driskoll peered up, but he couldn't see the face underneath the hood.

"That will be all, boy." Oswald pushed Driskoll aside and grabbed the doorframe, partially blocking Driskoll's view of the stranger.

"Can't get good help these days." Oswald sighed.

The stranger said nothing. Driskoll couldn't see much from

behind Oswald's hefty girth, but he did see a large gnarled hand reach out of the stranger's robes. The skin on the hand was a deep brown and it had a strange tattoo. Driskoll couldn't be sure, but he thought it looked like a small black dagger.

The hand held out a bottle of rose-colored liquid. Oswald took in a sharp breath as he spotted the bottle. "Celestial mead," he whispered. "Very rare."

The stranger's hood moved forward slightly, as if it were nodding. Oswald grabbed the bottle and ogled it. He turned to the stranger.

"That scroll you brought yesterday has been taken care of," Oswald said in a low voice.

Driskoll heard every word. The scroll the stranger had brought yesterday? Did Oswald mean the dagger scroll? The one that was in Driskoll's pocket right now?

Driskoll moved toward the door and squinted at the stranger. If he could only see who was behind that hood, he might know who had delivered it.

The stranger's hood turned and seemed to be facing Driskoll. Was it Driskoll's imagination or were eyes behind that hood, boring into him? Could they see the scroll hidden in his pocket?

He moved toward the door, but it slammed in his face. "And where do you think you're going?" the bard asked.

"Uh . . ."

Oswald looked at the bottle, and then at Driskoll. "Wait," he murmured. "I have a brilliant idea. Go back to the market and get me some more of that chocolate. It will go perfectly with my mead."

"But I can't pay—"

"Do not talk to me about trivial matters like money," Oswald shouted. "Tell them to put it on my tab. Now go!"

The bard muttered and turned away as Driskoll ran out the door. He looked up and down the street, but the stranger was gone.

Driskoll turned and headed for the market in Main Square. He walked slowly, thinking about the mysterious stranger. His dad had said there were a lot of strangers in town. Driskoll wondered if the stranger at the bard's had something to do with the castle.

When he arrived at the sweets stand, he noticed a knot of merchants had gathered around it. He recognized the butcher and the baker, but he'd never seen the tall, scowling man standing next to them. He was dressed in a black woolen tunic and leggings that matched his thick, ebony hair. Although it was a bit cold outside, he didn't wear any kind of jacket or cloak.

Driskoll gazed at the rows of chocolates in trays lining the counter. Which one should he get for Oswald?

"Can't say I've been to Promise Castle for years," the butcher said in his booming voice.

Driskoll looked up. Promise Castle?

"Place is a bit run down, isn't it?" the baker said.

"It's being rebuilt." The scowling man in black spoke in a low, gravelly voice. "I've been waiting for my workers, but many of them haven't arrived yet. I thought perhaps they had come through here."

His tanned face was wide and pockmarked, and his squinting black eyes darted from merchant to merchant.

Driskoll pretended to study the chocolate as the men murmured together.

"If you've got workers up there, they'll need to eat," said the elf maiden behind the counter. "I'll send one of my carts up tomorrow. Of course, it will cost you."

The stranger said nothing and walked away.

"Odd chap, isn't he?" the butcher said.

Driskoll forgot about the chocolate and followed the black-haired man. If he was looking for workers for Promise Castle, maybe he was heading there right now. The legend of the Dagger of Doom began at Promise Castle. And Ruida had said that the harpies had brought the Dagger of Doom to the castle. If he could find the castle, maybe he could find the dagger and save Kellach.

There can't be any harm in following him around and seeing what he's up to, Driskoll thought.

He kept a safe distance away from the man. He hid behind a cart and watched as the man stopped at the large stone obelisk in the center of Main Square. Shading his eyes from the sun, the man looked up at the needle-like tower and then down again. He reached out and rested his black-gloved hands on the obelisk's stone surface and kept them there for a minute or two. And then just as suddenly as he'd started, he dropped his hands and walked away.

Driskoll slipped out from behind the cart and followed.

The man stopped at the Cathedral of St. Cuthbert. Driskoll hid behind a statue and watched the man walking up and down the front steps, turning to look up at the tower and then frowning at the steps. He stopped at the cathedral wall and once again laid his gloved hands against it.

Driskoll was so absorbed in watching that he didn't realize he had moved away from the statue he'd been hiding behind. He was now standing on the stone steps not ten paces away.

The man stopped and headed down the steps. That was when Driskoll realized he was no longer hidden behind the statue. He turned and looked for the statue, but in the instant he looked away, the man was next to him, breathing hard. Before he could turn and run, the man reached out and grabbed Driskoll by the throat.

Driskoll struggled, but the man wrapped his hands tightly around Driskoll's neck, and his leather gloves burned against Driskoll's skin.

The man lifted Driskoll in the air, pulling him toward his reddened, scowling face. "I'll give you one chance to explain yourself, boy," he growled through sharp clenched teeth. "And then I'll decide whether or not you'll live."

CHAPTER

6

It seemed almost pointless to struggle. The man's grip was like iron, and the more Driskoll flailed his arms and legs, the tighter the hold became. A few more seconds and he would stop breathing forever.

"So tell me," the man whispered, "why you were following me."

"I—"

"What? Speak up."

"I—"

The stranger loosened his grip just enough for Driskoll to gurgle a reply.

"Work . . . I'm looking for work . . . castle."

"I don't hire children." The man tightened his grip again. "Except as slave labor. And I don't think you want to be one of my slaves."

Driskoll gagged.

"Now you listen to me." The man gave him another squeeze. "I don't like people sneaking around me. Next time, I'll—"

But he was interrupted by a sharp scream about two feet away. It startled him so much that he dropped Driskoll and whirled around.

That was Driskoll's chance. He broke free and tore away, following a patch of red hair running in front of him.

Moyra.

They rounded a corner and she slowed to a jog. "Did you like my diversion?"

"Thanks," Driskoll panted. They jumped over a low wall and onto another street. "But I could have taken care of myself."

"Yeah, right," she called over her shoulder. She finally stopped at a decrepit building, and they both looked around for the black-haired man. There was no sign of him anywhere.

"You can tell me who that was later," Moyra said. "Right now you need to come with me."

"Wait," Driskoll panted, rubbing his neck. "Let me rest a bit."

"No!" She grabbed his arm. "There's no time. I think Kellach's in trouble."

"What do you mean?"

"Come on, I'll show you." She started running again, and Driskoll raced after her. They ran through a narrow alley, scaring a couple of cat-sized rats that scurried away into the shadows.

"Where is Kellach?" Driskoll yelled.

But Moyra kept on running. She darted around a corner and up another alley. Two turns later, Driskoll found himself still behind her, in the Wizards' Quarter.

Moyra finally stopped at the beginning of a tiny row of shops. She pointed at a chalkboard sign halfway down the street that said: "Spider Leg Tea. Available in Tins or Catch it Yourself."

Behind the sign, wizards sat at little tables, drinking tea and eating sandwiches.

Driskoll glanced at them but turned back to her. "How come you're not out of breath?" he panted.

But Moyra put a finger to her lips and pointed again.

Driskoll turned and looked at the little café. "I don't see any—"

A skinny boy with long blonde hair and purple apprentice robes sat confidently rocking his chair at one of the tables. He was sipping something from a mug and chuckling at a joke he'd just made.

Another smaller figure in a brown cloak sat across from him, laughing. When Driskoll saw who the smaller figure was, he clamped his hand over his mouth.

"Kellach's not in trouble. He's just meeting a girl." His voice was muffled by his hand.

Then it dawned on Driskoll. That was where Kellach had gone the night before. He'd had a date with this girl. Driskoll smirked as he remembered how worried Kellach had been when he saw the scroll, afraid it would turn his hair into caterpillars. He didn't want to mess up his hair before his big date!

"Holy hags, Dris!" Moyra said. "Do I have to explain everything to you? If Kellach actually manages to convince this girl to be his girlfriend, there'll be trouble for sure."

"What kind of trouble?"

"Are you kidding me?" Moyra threw up her hands. "Kellach'll be unbearable! You think he's full of himself now? Just wait until he—"

Kellach looked up. He had spotted them.

"Oh great," Driskoll muttered. "I'll never hear the end of this."

Kellach threw a few coppers on the table and sauntered over to them. The girl stumbled at his side. Driskoll pretended he had just noticed Kellach.

"Oh, *er,* hi, Kellach. Fancy meeting you here."

Kellach ignored Driskoll's polite wave. "What are you two doing here?"

Moyra opened her mouth to say something but closed it again. Neither of them had an answer. Driskoll just stared at the girl.

"Never mind," Kellach said, turning to the girl. "Willeona, I know you'll find this hard to believe but these two rude and immature people are the only other Knights of the Silver Dragon alive besides Zendric and me. This is Moyra. And this is my little brother, Driskoll."

Kellach held out his hand to present the girl. "This," he said with a little wave of his hand, "is Willeona Renwood."

The girl's large amber eyes darted from Driskoll to Moyra. "Good afternoon," she said softly, without smiling.

There was a long awkward silence as they all stared at one another. Driskoll couldn't help but stare at a small, round locket that she wore around her neck. It looked like a tiny mirror.

"What's that?" He pointed at the mirror around her neck.

She looked down at Driskoll. He could have sworn her eyes darkened from gold to brown to black. "I took this from someone who crossed me once. He will never do it again."

"Who was it?" Driskoll asked quietly.

"It's none of your business." Kellach shot a nasty look at Driskoll and turned to Willeona. "Come on, let's go. These children don't know how to act in public."

Willeona nodded at Driskoll and Moyra and followed Kellach. She stumbled a little, and Kellach caught her. Then they did something so completely disgusting that Driskoll had to look away.

They giggled.

CHAPTER

7

L et's get out of here," Driskoll said.

Moyra watched Kellach and Willeona walk away. "Clumsy, isn't she?"

"Come on, Moyra."

She shook herself. "All right," she said. "But there's just something about seeing Kellach with that girl that makes me feel sick."

"Oh no." Driskoll slapped his forehead. "Speaking of feeling sick, I was supposed to bring chocolate back to Old Oswald an hour ago! He's going to give me another cursed scroll if I don't get back soon." Driskoll started jogging toward Main Square.

Moyra caught up to him. "Wait. You never told me. Who was that guy in the square? He looked like he was going to squeeze the life out of you."

"I thought he was too. He's building the castle."

"What castle?"

Driskoll explained what his father had told him about the castle being built, and about how he had overheard the black-haired man say he was looking for workers for Promise Castle.

"But you already have a job. What does that have to do with you?"

"Don't you remember the story of the Dagger of Doom?" Driskoll asked. "The brothers in the story lived in Promise Castle."

"You're kind of going crazy over that old drawing, aren't you?" Moyra asked. "You don't even know if the real dagger exists."

"It does," Driskoll said simply.

"How do you know?"

"Well for one thing, Ruida told me today that she stole it."

"Hold it. Who's Ruida?"

They were back in Main Square. Driskoll looked over his shoulder for the black- haired stranger. Then he explained about Ruida and how she'd said the dagger in the drawing looked just like the one she'd stolen.

"Hmm, Moyra said. "It shouldn't take a whole flock of harpies to steal a tiny little dagger." She paused and straightened. "Not that I would know anything about stealing."

Driskoll grinned. "No, of course you wouldn't."

"But you said they flew back to the city, and she crashed into Zendric's tower," she continued. "Why would harpies come here? You'd think they would want to take the dagger back to their nest in the ruins. So why would they fly to Curston?" Moyra shook her head. "Harpies never come here. They don't like to risk getting hit by the watchers' arrows. That's one of the few things that can kill them."

"So why would they risk their lives to fly back to the city?" Driskoll said.

"The only reason people steal anything and don't hide it right away is if they're delivering it to someone else," Moyra said thoughtfully.

"Exactly," Driskoll said. "Ruida said something about the castle. I think they were taking it there."

They arrived at the sweets stand.

"Sorry, I just sold my last batch of fudge," the elf maiden said when Driskoll asked.

Driskoll looked desperately at the pies and sweet breads. "Do you have anything that's chocolate?"

"Nope," the elf maiden said. "How about a nice mince pie?"

Driskoll shook his head. "No, thanks."

Moyra snickered. "You are in so much trouble."

∎ ∎ ∎ ∎ ∎

"I think I'll wait outside for a few minutes," Moyra said when they arrived at Oswald's house. She sat down on the front steps. "Let me know if you need me."

"I won't need your help," Driskoll mumbled, climbing the stone steps toward the bard's front door. But he didn't ask her to leave. It was nice knowing that he had some backup as he faced the bard without the eagerly awaited chocolate.

Driskoll opened the front door expecting to be greeted by the usual sounds of the bard grumbling and scrolls shuffling. But he didn't hear anything. As he walked from the front room to the bard's study, he pictured being pelted with scrolls.

But the study was empty. Driskoll looked in the kitchen, but Oswald wasn't there either. He checked the back garden. The cleaning cauldron sat empty among the weeds.

Driskoll went back inside. There was one more room in the bard's house that he hadn't checked: Oswald's bedroom.

Driskoll curled his lip at the thought of going in the room where the bard actually slept. He had never been in there, nor had he had any desire to. For some reason, he had always pictured it as a large and filthy rat's nest made of shredded scrolls and scraps of old food.

The door to the bedroom was open. Driskoll held his breath and peeked in.

He was relieved to see that it was just a normal bedroom with a normal, though very large, bed. A big gray lump, its middle rising and falling rhythmically, nestled in the center of the bed.

Oswald was fast asleep. Dirty plates and scraps of food littered the floor next to the bed, and amid it all, lay the empty bottle of celestial mead.

CHAPTER

8

Moyra looked up in surprise as Driskoll bounded down toward the street.

"What, no black eye?" she asked. "No cursed scrolls?"

"Nope. He's asleep," Driskoll said.

"Asleep? In the middle of the day?"

"I think he ate himself sick."

Moyra scrunched up her nose in disgust.

"Come on." Driskoll ran ahead. "This means I'm free! We can go find Promise Castle."

"Are you crazy?" She pulled him back. "You said that creepy stranger is building it. Why would we want to go anywhere near him?"

"Well, we have to go to the castle if I'm going to find this dagger," he said as he pulled out the dagger drawing and looked at it. There was Kellach's name on it again. He shivered.

Suddenly a hand clasped his shoulder. Driskoll jumped and wheeled around. It was Kellach.

"Aren't you supposed to be cleaning scrolls right now?" Kellach asked.

"Oswald's sleeping," Driskoll said. "So, I guess that means I'm free for the day. What are you doing here?"

"You two looked like you were up to no good a while ago, so I thought I'd keep you out of trouble," Kellach said.

"You've got it backward, Kellach. I'm the one keeping you out of trouble," Driskoll answered. "You're the one whose name is on the dagger."

"Whatever." Kellach looked away.

Moyra smirked. "So where's your girlfriend?"

Kellach went red. "She's not my girlfriend," he muttered. "And anyway, she had to go home. Where are you two going?"

"We're going to the Old Quarter. They're building a castle there," Moyra said. "Driskoll thinks it's got something to do with his dagger drawing."

Kellach rolled his eyes but he walked with them.

Driskoll kept looking over his shoulder for the black-haired man, but so far there was no sign of him.

"So what are we looking for?" Moyra asked.

"Dunno." Driskoll shrugged. "I guess a place that looks like there's going to be a castle built on it."

"And what would that look like?" Driskoll ignored the sarcasm in Kellach's voice.

"I'm not sure exactly," he answered. "I've never seen a castle being built before."

They walked down the street, past Watchers' Hall, to the very end of the roadway. Ahead of them lay the Westgate, surrounded

45

by watchers. To the left, a dirt road ran along the inside of the city wall.

Kellach stopped and peered down the dirt road. "I don't see how anyone could build a castle here. There's no room! Are you *sure* you heard Dad right?"

"Yes!" Driskoll said. "Dad said they're building a castle in the Old Quarter, so I know it's got to be around here. And the elf at the sweets stand told the black-haired man that she'd send her cart *up* there. I wonder if they're building it on a hill somewhere."

"That makes sense," Moyra said, as they began walking down the dirt road. "You'd want to build a castle on a hill so you could see your enemies coming."

"There's one problem," Kellach cut in. "There are no hills in Curston."

As they turned the corner, Moyra pointed ahead of them. "What's that?"

A tiny grove of three pine trees stood at the end of the road. Above the trees, they could see the tops of a few more trees. They looked like they were set further back, and higher than the others.

Moyra shrugged. "Looks like a hill to me."

"I've never noticed that before," Driskoll murmured.

"I have," Kellach said. "That's Cor's Rise. It's just a tiny patch of land. It bumps right up against the city wall and the Phoenix Quarter. It's nothing."

"*Cor's* Rise?" Driskoll's eyes widened. "Cor is one of the brothers from the legend of the dagger!"

"Yeah," Kellach said. "But I'm sure it's just a coincidence—"

But Driskoll had already taken off. He followed the dirt road

46

until it came to the small hill. The trees were growing within a few feet from one another, and the spaces in between were threaded with thick vines. He walked along the grove's edge, not knowing exactly what he was looking for.

"This is nothing," Kellach said, catching up. "It's just a little hill. You couldn't fit a chimney on top of this thing."

But Driskoll stopped. There was a small opening in between two of the trees where the vines had been cut back.

"Look," he said, picking up a branch and pointing at the sharp break on it. "This was cut in the last few days."

Moyra peered in between the trees. "There's a path." She pointed at a long, narrow clearing.

"Let's go." Driskoll started forward.

"Hold it," Kellach said. "You don't know what's in there."

"You said yourself that it was nothing, Kellach. It can't hurt to check it out."

Kellach nodded stiffly. "All right," he said. "But keep your eyes open."

Driskoll didn't need to be told. He could still feel the black-haired man's hands around his neck. He looked all around him at the trees on either side of the path. They were tall and so thickly spaced that there was very little sunlight. But there were signs of vines and branches that had been cut recently, and someone had piled leaves all along the sides of the path.

They climbed for about twenty minutes, following the twisting trail.

"This is impossible," Kellach panted. "How can there be so much land here?"

"It must be magic," Moyra said.

The path finally ended in front of a crumbling stone wall.

"Well, we've finally reached the wall," Kellach said. "And as I told you, there's nothing here."

Driskoll looked along the wall. Vines had been cut away from it, and it looked like the path continued along the wall in both directions. But there was something wrong. It didn't look like the rest of the city wall.

Moyra was standing behind him, looking back over the path they had just traveled on. She spun around. "Have you seen this view?"

Driskoll turned and looked.

All of Curston lay below him. He could see Zendric's tower and the Cathedral of St. Cuthbert. He could see the roof of his own house.

"How come we can't see this hill from the city? Moyra asked. "It's huge."

"Haven't got a clue," Kellach said.

Driskoll sat on a rock and studied the wall. There was definitely something strange about it.

"I can see everything from up here, and I don't see any big construction sites," Kellach said.

Driskoll ignored him. He picked up a stone and absently tossed it at the wall.

"Maybe the construction hasn't started yet," Moyra suggested.

Driskoll jumped up as a stone fell into his lap.

He looked at Kellach. "Hey, quit it."

"What?" Kellach asked.

Driskoll narrowed his eyes. "Don't pretend you don't know about the rock you just threw at me."

"I didn't throw anything." Kellach frowned.

Driskoll looked at the wall. He picked up the rock and threw it at the wall again. Instead of glancing off the wall and falling, the rock sailed back and landed flat on the ground in front of him.

"How did it do that?" Driskoll asked in amazement.

Kellach ran his hands across the wall, puzzling over it. "This isn't the city wall."

Driskoll looked up and down the structure. The top of it was broken off as if a giant hand had swiped at it.

Farther along the path that ran along it, he could see a huge pile of rubble, where it looked like part of the wall had been blasted away.

"There are no broken sections of the city wall," Kellach murmured as they began walking along it.

"And if this were the city wall," Driskoll said, "the other side would be . . . would be . . ."

"It wouldn't be Curston, that's for sure." Kellach said. "It would be the land beyond Curston."

"And it wouldn't be this," Moyra said when they got to the rubble that lay around the broken down section of the wall.

There, was an opening in the wall several feet across, enough for at least four people to climb through, side by side. It opened into a wide, overgrown area that looked like it had been centuries since it had seen visitors.

Tall weeds grew in between huge, fallen boulders. Broken statues and chunks of stone lay scattered on the ground. The only thing resembling a building was a stone archway directly ahead of them and in the center of the clearing. Long wooden planks lay in shreds all around the archway, covering the weedy ground.

They walked across the clearing and stood in front of the archway.

"Looks like an ancient ruin," Moyra said, lifting one of the smaller boards with her foot and letting it fall. The rotten plank landed with a thud and splintered.

"Or an ancient tomb," Driskoll added, shivering. "It's awfully quiet."

"So how come we've never seen this before?" Moyra asked.

"I don't know," Kellach answered. "It's impossible that all of this would fit on this little hill."

"I'm confused," Moyra said. "Your dad said they're building a castle. But this one looks like it's been torn down."

"Wait a minute." Driskoll looked at her. "The black-haired man said he was rebuilding it. Don't you see? This *is* Promise Castle. It's not a construction site we should have been looking for. We're looking for ruins!"

Kellach snorted. "This is your castle? This is nothing but a moldy old rock pile."

Moyra gasped. "Look at that." She pointed into the archway at some twisted iron bars. The twisted bars cast weird shadows on the ground in the late afternoon light.

"I think this might have been a door at one time," Kellach said.

"You're right," Driskoll answered. Looks like this was the entrance. All of this wood might have been a drawbridge across a moat. And the portcullis was just beyond."

"The port-what?" Moyra asked.

"The portcullis. Those big iron bars. You could pull them up and down. They protected the door."

"Looks like they weren't very much help here," Kellach said, touching a rusty bar that looked like it might crumble any second.

"Something terrible must have happened here," Driskoll said.

"I bet it was those mantelpieces," Moyra muttered.

"Mantlehorn," Driskoll corrected, still peering through the archway. He thought he saw a shadow move inside, but he blinked and it was gone.

Moyra's eyes grew wide. "Someone's watching us. I can feel it."

Driskoll felt a shiver crawl down his spine.

"All right," Kellach said. "You've seen enough. Let's go."

"But I thought we were going to go inside," Driskoll said, "into the ruins."

"Look," Kellach wheeled around and faced him. "There are ruins on the outside of town. And have you ever been inside them and not almost been killed?"

"But these aren't the same—"

"Ruins are ruins," Kellach said. "They're dangerous. And you're not going in there."

"Oh really?" Driskoll asked. "Says who?"

"Says me." Kellach crossed his arms.

Driskoll frowned. "Nobody asked you to come, Kellach."

"I'm here only to keep you out of trouble," Kellach muttered. "If Zendric knew we were here and that I was not studying spells, he'd turn both of us into chew toys for that pet harpy of his. And by the way, did you feed her today?"

51

Driskoll suddenly remembered his promise to bring Ruida more meat. "Yeah," he said, grasping his throat at the thought of the violence with which she shook her cage.

"Hmmpf," Kellach said. He looked at the stone arch and then back at Driskoll, a wisecracking grin spreading across his face. "Well anyway, you're the one she likes," he continued. "You and your lovely bard voice."

"What are you talking about?" Driskoll asked.

Kellach tucked his fists into his armpits and stuck out his elbows to make it look like he had wings. "Oh, Mister Bardman," he squawked. "Please tell Ruida another sto-o-o-ry."

Driskoll scowled. How did Kellach know about that?

"When you two old hags stop arguing, let me know. I'm leaving." Moyra bounded down the path through the trees.

"Kellach, why don't you just leave too?" Driskoll started walking toward the ruined castle door. "I'm going to poke around more. And see if I can find something about that dagger."

Driskoll tried to concentrate on looking for clues, but Kellach stood behind him, laughing and hooting, "Mr. Bardman has such a lovely voice."

Driskoll looked at the rotting wood planks on the ground in front of the doorway.

"Mr. Bardman, tell Ruida another story, or she'll eat you!" Kellach taunted.

"Shut up, Kellach." Driskoll jumped over a broken beam and landed on a spongy wood plank.

He didn't hear the change in Kellach's voice. He never heard his brother's warning.

"Driskoll! Watch out!"

It was too late.

The soft wooden planks beneath Driskoll had already begun to give way. He could do nothing but stare at the stone archway above him as he slipped through the rotting boards.

Suddenly everything was black.

CHAPTER

9

"Oof." Driskoll landed with a painful thud on a mud floor. He shut his eyes and covered his head as the avalanche of crashing wood came down with him, followed by a stream of moldy wood flakes and tiny stones.

Pebbles and dust fell for what seemed like hours, but Driskoll kept his eyes shut tight. He was certain he had dodged the wooden beams that had toppled around him, although he didn't know how.

Once everything had settled, he blinked a few times, but the view was the same: dark nothingness.

Driskoll wondered if maybe a plank had caught him and he really was dead. He tried to move. First his legs and then his arms. Everything seemed to be working, except his eyes. Maybe I went blind, he thought.

"Driskoll? Dris? Are you there? Are you okay?" he heard Kellach calling through the darkness.

"Yeah," was all Driskoll could manage to say as he rubbed the spot on his shoulder where a stone had pelted him. He strained his eyes, but all he could see was black.

He smelled something too. Moldy wood and something else. Something foul and familiar.

"Where are you?" Kellach called.

Driskoll grunted in reply.

"Can you give me a hand?" Kellach asked. "I think I'm stuck."

Driskoll got up slowly and turned in the direction of Kellach's voice. "Where are you?"

"Right here."

Kellach was a few paces away. Driskoll stepped over some beams until he heard Kellach breathing right below him.

"The floor started to seal up right after you went down," Kellach said. "I didn't know what was going to happen to you, so I went in after you." There was a note of fear in his voice. "But now I think my leg is stuck."

"Have you got a torch?" Driskoll asked.

Kellach scoffed. "I didn't bring any supplies. I didn't think we'd need any for a walk through town."

Driskoll knelt and felt around until he touched Kellach's leg and the wooden beam laying across it.

"Can't you do a spell or something to lift it?"

"I tried," Kellach said, "but it's not working. There's some strange kind of magic that's blocking my spells down here. See if you can move it off me."

Driskoll was tugging at the beam when he heard something. A low, wheezing, rattling kind of sound.

"Did you hear that?"

"Ow," Kellach grunted. "This beam hurts. Get it off me!"

The sound was getting louder. Something was dragging itself along the floor toward them.

Driskoll could see nothing in the flat black void. He pulled on the wooden beam again, but it didn't budge.

"Come on, Driskoll! I can't do this alone."

"I'm trying!"

The thing dragging itself on the ground was getting closer.

Driskoll pulled with all of his might, and the beam slowly inched upward. He heard Kellach scrambling out. Kellach grabbed him, and they ran blindly until they hit a wall. The noisy breathing was behind them, getting closer.

Kellach scratched at the wall. "There's nothing here—wait." Driskoll heard a slight groan as Kellach heaved himself up.

"It's a ledge," Kellach whispered. "Climb up."

Driskoll felt the wall. The creature was almost at his side. Something whispered in his ear.

"Hungry," it rasped.

Frantically, he felt the wall, but there was nothing to grasp.

"Put your foot right here," Kellach called from above him. Driskoll put his hand directly under the area where he had heard Kellach's voice.

Something sharp glided down his back just as he found the crevice in the wall. He yelped and stuck his foot in the crack, scrambling up the wall faster than he had ever moved in his life.

The ledge was wide enough for them both. The creature scratched at the wall, trying to heave itself up.

"I don't know how long we'll last up here," Kellach panted. "That thing wants to get us."

The creature grunted and scratched.

Driskoll sniffed. "Wait! I smell fresh air." Driskoll laid his hands on the wall.

He found a small stone outcropping and pushed himself up. Just above him was another. "We can climb up, Kellach. I think it leads somewhere." Driskoll looked up and thought he could see a glimmer of sunlight.

"Didn't I tell you?" Kellach said as they felt their way up the wall. "Didn't I tell you to stay out of the ruins? Ruins are dangerous, I said. But would you listen?"

This was one of those times when Driskoll wished he were the apprentice wizard and not Kellach. He occupied his mind trying to think of what he would turn Kellach into if he could. A baby duck? A meat pie? Maybe he would just turn him into a rock and throw him back into the moat. Then he could be done with him.

It was getting brighter, and soon Driskoll could see an opening above them. He poked his head through and looked out at a small, rectangular room. There were some overturned benches on one end and a small stone platform on the other. Moyra sat down on the platform, looking at him as if he'd just dropped in for lunch.

"Looks like you missed the shortcut," she said.

CHAPTER

10

Driskoll heaved himself onto the stone floor and lay on his back for a moment, looking around. Kellach followed. There was nothing in the room. A wooden door flanked one wall. Next to it was a large, oval window. Its glass was cracked and dirty.

"Where did you come from?" Driskoll asked Moyra. "I thought you left!"

"I did," Moyra said. "But as I was walking down the path, I heard you and Kellach shouting. I ran back up here, but you were both gone. When I started looking for you, I found this building."

"What is this place?" Kellach asked. "I don't remember seeing any buildings when we were searching the area earlier."

"Amazing," Driskoll breathed. "It must be more magic."

"If you think this is amazing, you should look outside," Moyra said, getting up and leading them to the cracked window.

Driskoll found himself staring at the open area they had seen from the other side of the archway. But there was something else there now. Something they hadn't seen before. Directly across from them, a majestic stone tower rose at least a hundred feet in the air. It was a simple circular shape, with a few slit windows here and there. Its roof had been destroyed, but the main part of the tower was still intact.

Driskoll's mouth dropped open. "That was definitely not here when we came up here," he whispered.

"Neither was this little building," Moyra said.

"How could we not see two buildings?" Driskoll asked.

"Maybe it's a good thing I came with you after all." Kellach turned to Driskoll. "You would never have found this place alone."

"What?" Driskoll threw up his hands. "If it hadn't been for me, you'd never have found this place."

"If it hadn't been for me," Kellach said, looking down his nose at Driskoll, "you'd have been eaten alive in that stinking moat."

"I found a way up the wall," Driskoll said. "I got us up here."

"You seem to have forgotten that I was the one who got you up the ledge," Kellach said.

Moyra stood in between them. "What's gotten into you two? All you've done since we've been here is fight."

"His fault," Driskoll grumbled, pointing at Kellach.

Moyra threw her hands in the air. "You two are impossible! I'm going to go explore the tower." She walked out the tiny door and into the courtyard.

"Okay, if you're so smart," Driskoll said, tapping his toes and looking up at his brother, "how come we didn't see these two buildings when we came up here?"

Kellach looked past Driskoll to the window beyond him.

"Dunno." Kellach shrugged.

Driskoll smirked. "There's magic all over this place, and you can't even see it. When we fell into the moat and the roof closed up—"

"Correction," Kellach interrupted. "You fell into the moat. I jumped in after you. I just had an unfortunate accident while trying to save you. But you're right, there's some kind of strange magic going on."

"Yeah," Driskoll said excitedly. "Now if we could only figure out what happened here. There must have been some kind of battle . . ." He went on excitedly while Kellach looked around.

"Do you think it happened during the Sundering of the Seal?" Driskoll asked. "I wonder—"

"If you would just stop talking for a minute, I could think," Kellach interrupted. "I need to figure out what's going on with the magic here."

But Driskoll just kept talking. "I wonder what it will look like when it's rebuilt. Maybe it'll have more towers and huge battlements. I bet they'll put in a dungeon with dragons in it or something."

"Can't you stop talking for one minute?" Kellach asked.

"You can't tell me what to do," Driskoll said defiantly. "I'm sick of you ordering me around. Why don't you just *not* listen to me? You're good at that. You've been doing it all day."

"I know you're saying that to annoy me, Driskoll. And it's working." Kellach drummed his fingers on the wall. "Now could you please shut up? I'm trying to think."

Driskoll ignored him. "Did you know that it can take forty years to build a castle? They're fascinating places, really . . ."

Kellach narrowed his eyes. "Maybe you need something to make you stop talking." Kellach looked at him and raised his hands in the air, muttering.

"This must have been some kind of guardhouse," Driskoll said. "Wait! What are you doing?"

Driskoll suddenly felt a slight tickle in his throat. Kellach was staring at him expectantly.

Clearing his throat, Driskoll tried to say something. "What did you do?" He could hear someone else talking in an unbearably loud, shrill voice. "And who is screaming?"

Kellach frowned at him.

"What did you do?" Driskoll cried again. The shrill voice, he realized, was his own.

The window behind them shattered.

"Oops," Kellach said quietly. "That was supposed to be a silencing spell. Something's really messing with magic in here. He looked at Driskoll and stifled a laugh. "But I'll have to remember this one."

"It isn't funny," Driskoll shrieked in a voice that sounded something like the squeal of a mouse, but about fifty times louder. Another window shattered somewhere in the distance.

Kellach shrugged and stepped over the glass shards. "You were asking for it."

Driskoll shook with anger. "That's it," he shouted. "I saved you from that thing in the moat, and this is the thanks I get."

He stomped out the door and ran into the open area. He thought about looking for Moyra and began picking his way through the stones toward the tower when he heard someone yelling behind him.

"Hey!"

Driskoll stopped. It was Kellach.

Just keep going, he thought. But there was something like fear in Kellach's voice. Driskoll turned back.

So help me, Kellach, he thought, if this is another of your jokes . . .

Driskoll ran into the tiny guardhouse. Kellach was staring at something stuck in the wall.

"It came right through the door," Kellach said, pointing at the shiny object. "Someone threw it at me. But I moved and it missed."

Driskoll looked at the shining silver handle of a dagger. It was carved with the emblem of the Knights of the Silver Dragon.

Kellach reached up and slowly pried it out of the wall. He held it up and stared at it.

Driskoll could see the familiar but strange runes on the guard, and his own stunned expression staring back at him from the mirror-like blade.

And he could see the seven letters burned into it: KELLACH.

CHAPTER

11

"Nice joke, Dris," Kellach said, smiling. "We're even now."

Driskoll didn't hear him. "It's here," he shrieked. "I was right! The dagger is real."

Moyra ran inside. "I heard screaming. What's going on?" Her eyes widened at the sight of the dagger in Kellach's hands. "What in the name of dragon fire is that?"

"Ask Driskoll," Kellach said. "It came at me right after he left."

Driskoll was barely listening. "The Dagger of Doom," he shrieked. "I knew it."

Moyra grimaced and covered her ears. "What happened to your voice?"

But Driskoll didn't care anymore. "Look at it, Kellach. I told you it existed," he shrieked.

"Kellach," Moyra said, "do us all a favor and fix his voice, will you?"

Kellach shook his head. "I'm not doing any more magic in this place. Something is really weird around here." He looked at

Driskoll. "Besides, the spell will wear off after a few minutes."

Driskoll still wasn't listening. "Will you just look at this dagger? Have you ever seen anything like it?" His voice was still loud, though not as high-pitched.

"It's amazing," Moyra said breathlessly. "It's like . . . it's like a mirror."

Kellach was still holding it in both hands, staring at his own reflection all around his name.

"Creepy." Moyra shuddered.

Driskoll nodded. "And look at those runes on the hilt."

He pulled out the dagger drawing and held it up to the real dagger in Kellach's hands.

But Moyra stared at the drawing. "It's the same," she said, looking at Driskoll in amazement.

Driskoll nodded. "The runes are much clearer on the real dagger." They gazed at the strange runes for a moment.

≈Vi⌖ ⁊≈⋂W◈

Kellach traced the runes on the dagger with his finger. "That's not any language I've ever heard of. They're meaningless."

Kellach suddenly rolled his eyes. He shook the dagger at Driskoll with a grin on his face.

"Right," he said, "you had me scared for a moment, Dris, but the joke's over now."

Moyra turned to Kellach. "Oh come on, Kellach. You don't really still think Driskoll did this, do you?"

"Of course," he said. "He's been mad at me about the butterflies in his hair, and then I performed that little spell that, uh . . . , changed his voice. But we're even now since he tried to attack me with this knife."

Driskoll, who had been staring at the dagger in disbelief, finally heard what Kellach was saying. "It's not a knife, it's a dagger." His normal voice had almost completely returned. "And I didn't do it. Ruida said the harpies stole this dagger. They delivered it to someone in the city. If we could just figure out who they brought it to, we'd know who threw it at you. Don't you get it, Kellach? Someone wants to *kill* you!"

"Great story, Driskoll," Kellach said, sweeping the dagger through the air. "And this dagger is pretty good. Nice and heavy. Realistic. What is it, a prop from one of the stories Oswald tells? Did you pull it out of his closet when he wasn't looking?"

"That's no prop, Kellach," Moyra said quietly.

Kellach looked from Moyra to his brother. "Okay, Driskoll, if you didn't throw it at me, who did?" He pointed the dagger at Moyra. "You?"

She stared at him calmly. "Maybe you should ask the person who lives here if he knows about it."

"Okay," Kellach said, glancing down at the dagger. "Maybe I—" He looked up at her. "What did you say?"

"Come on, I'll show you." She led the two boys outside and pointed at the tower. "While you orc brains were screaming at each other, I was up here checking the place out. And I found out that somebody lives here."

Kellach shrugged. "All right, I'll spend five minutes looking for this person, but then I'm out of here."

He started toward the tower, but Moyra grabbed his arm. "Quiet," she hissed. "Someone's watching us."

Driskoll shivered. He felt it too. Someone, or something, was nearby. He looked around expecting to see the black-haired man jumping out at them from behind a boulder. But instead, he seemed to be seeing everything through a murky haze. Kellach and Moyra were a bit blurry, and they seemed to be moving very slowly. Was he dreaming? What was going on here?

And then, something very odd happened.

A large brown deer walked through the stone archway and crept up to Kellach. The deer had a plain brown coat, and its striking golden eyes gazed at the older boy's face.

Driskoll felt powerless to move or say anything. The deer nudged Kellach, and the dagger dropped out of his hand. The deer gently took the blade in its teeth and then backed up slowly, still watching Kellach. Then it bolted through the archway and disappeared.

Driskoll shook himself, and everything returned to normal.

"Did you see that?" Driskoll asked. "Am I crazy, or did a deer just come up and take that dagger from you?"

Kellach nodded, looking in the direction it had run off.

"We have to go and get that dagger back, Kellach," he yelled.

"No," Kellach said, putting a hand on his shoulder. "No. She's supposed to have it."

"What?" Driskoll asked. "How do you know?"

"I don't—I don't know. You'll just have to trust me on this one."

Driskoll looked at Kellach. There was something strange going on, and he didn't like this at all.

Moyra was watching Kellach too. "That was really weird,

Kellach. Maybe we should leave."

"No," he said, looking at them both. "It's okay, really. Come on. Let's go find this person who lives here."

Moyra and Driskoll hung back.

"This place is really weird," Moyra whispered to Driskoll as they walked toward the tower. "It's doing things to all of us."

"Kellach said he couldn't do magic when we were in the moat," Driskoll whispered back. "And let's not forget that buildings are appearing out of thin air."

"And that deer," Moyra muttered. "Did you feel like you were looking at it from far away or something?"

Driskoll nodded.

"It looked very familiar," Moyra said. "There was something about it . . ."

"Hey you two," Kellach called back to them. He stood at the base of the tower, facing a half-open door. He peered in.

Driskoll looked over Kellach's shoulder. The door opened into a landing. Ahead of them lay a spiral staircase.

"Come on," Kellach said, disappearing inside.

They followed him up, careful not to trip on the little scraps of torn parchment and moldy apple cores littering the steps.

At the top of the staircase, a door loomed in front of them. Before Driskoll could say anything, Kellach opened it and peeked into the room beyond.

"Have you ever heard of knocking?" Driskoll whispered loudly. "You don't know who's—"

"It's okay, no one's in here," Kellach whispered back. Moyra and Driskoll followed him into a strange circular room. Driskoll wasn't sure if it actually had walls, or if it was the thousands of tools and knives hanging from hooks that were holding up the roof. Every inch of wall space was covered with tools—sickles, mallets, saws, and several rather barbaric-looking devices that Driskoll couldn't identify.

The room itself was a confused maze of trestle tables overflowing with building models, piles of scrolls, and a few half-eaten meat pies. Scattered in between the tables were tottering columns of books. And high above the mess, a wire and feather contraption suspended from the ceiling.

Driskoll was gazing at its batlike parchment wings when a voice from the door made him freeze.

The voice boomed, "I'll pound you with every ounce of strength I have when I find you."

CHAPTER

12

A lanky, white-haired man clanked through the doorway. He wore a dirty leather apron with deep pockets overflowing with hammers, rulers, and some other strange tools. With every long, ungainly step the old man took, it sounded like an entire toolbox chinked along with him.

He hurried to a column of books and plucked one from the bottom of the stack, causing twenty others to fall on him. Without looking away from his book, he reached for a gray half-eaten sandwich on the table next to him and took a big bite.

Driskoll didn't want to guess the age of the sandwich or the man's.

He could see that Moyra and Kellach were just as awestruck as he was, maybe more.

The old man turned to them suddenly, his mouth half full of sandwich. "Apprentice builders don't lollygag around," he growled. "You think castle construction is a party? And where are my nails? I'll pound them when I find them."

Kellach finally composed himself. "Excuse us, sir."

69

The old man fixed on Kellach with a threatening glare that made him seem to shrink.

"Hey old man," Moyra said. "You see anyone with a dagger around here?"

"Eh?" He peered at her for a few minutes, and his eyes softened. "You aren't building apprentices, are you?" He slapped his forehead, leaving a greasy black mark. "Don't get many visitors these days. Used to know all about entertaining guests."

Moyra wasn't backing down. "I said, did you see anyone with a dagger?"

"Dagger? What kind of dagger?"

"The Dagger of Doom," Driskoll blurted.

Kellach and Moyra gave him looks that said "keep your mouth shut," but the old man sat and mumbled. "The Dagger of Doom. Means death to anyone whose name appears on the blade."

"Well, it appeared today with my brother's name on it," Driskoll said. Kellach stepped hard on Driskoll's toe.

The old man bounded across the room.

"And then a deer stole it," Driskoll continued.

He dropped a hammer loudly. "Stole it?" the old man said angrily. "That was no deer! That was a mantlehorn. Thieving, conniving creatures."

"That was a mantlehorn?" Driskoll asked excitedly.

"Of course," he said. "They can change from a deer to a human at will. Dangerous creatures," he said, his eyes shifting from side to side. "And while the mantlehorn have a dagger with your name on it, you are in danger."

"Creatures that change into deer don't sound very dangerous," Kellach muttered under his breath.

The old man looked at Kellach. "Who are you again?"

"I'm Kellach, and this is my brother, Driskoll. We're sons of Torin. Captain of the watch."

The old man regarded them for a moment. "Torin, eh? Captain of the watch? Hmm . . . And who is your mother?"

"This is our friend, Moyra," Kellach said, working hard to get off the subject of their missing mother. "We were exploring these ruins and we stumbled on your—your . . ."

"My home," he said with an awkward swish of his arm. "Welcome to Hadrian's attic. I'm Hadrian. This is where I create inventions, buildings, and ah, other, ah . . . things."

His wrist had become caught in the wire and feather contraption hanging from the ceiling. As he shook his arm to untangle himself, the gadget fell to the floor and collapsed. Hadrian stepped over the mess and began guiding the kids across the room, taking long detours around piles of books and tools and chicken bones.

Driskoll momentarily forgot about the dagger as he looked at the wonders of Hadrian's attic. Most of the inventions were fascinating, like the floor-cleaning shoes and the doghouse made out of steak bones. Others were downright strange, like the scale model of a house with built-in spiderwebs for trapping bugs. Driskoll shivered as a very large and very hairy black leg poked out one of the windows.

"So how come we haven't heard about this place?" Kellach asked.

"This place?" Hadrian asked. "You mean Promise Castle? Well, at one time everyone had heard of it. People came from miles around just to see it." He winked. "Or not see it."

71

"Huh?"

"Invisibility spell," he said. "The whole place disappeared when enemies approached. In its prime, it could make itself look taller and bigger than it really was."

"Well, that explains a few things," Moyra muttered.

"This castle is like no other," Hadrian continued. "Sorcerers built it centuries ago. They put a powerful magic into it. When it was destroyed, much of that magic left. It was as if the spirit of the magic died. And I think the old castle was embarrassed at the state it was in. It didn't want anyone to see it, so it just disappeared completely."

"How was it destroyed?"

Hadrian looked sadly at the walls. "Ah, that was the work of the Knight of Mirrors," he said in a deep, sorrowful voice. He trailed off.

Driskoll broke the silence. "But the castle's reappearing now because it's being rebuilt, right?"

"Now how do you know about that?" Hadrian raised his white eyebrows.

"I heard someone talking about it in the marketplace," Driskoll said.

"Must have been Scraper," he said. "My master mason." He pointed at a patched cloth covering something large on a table.

"What's that?" Kellach asked.

Hadrian looked at Kellach as if he'd just said a foul word. "What's this? Why, it's Promise Castle, boy."

"Oh." Kellach looked puzzled

Hadrian removed the cloth, revealing a scale model of a castle.

72

"Ohhh," the kids all said at once. "That's the castle."

It was a very detailed model. There were many towers and buildings surrounded by a high wall. "That's what this place is going to look like when we're finished."

Hadrian looked at his model as if he were looking at a favorite grandchild. "I've been waiting a lifetime for the right tools," he said. He looked at Kellach for a few seconds. "Construction begins tomorrow."

Driskoll eyed the model suspiciously. "There aren't any giant spiderwebs or anything of the sort in it, are there?"

Hadrian chuckled. "No, but we've got work ahead of us. Castle construction is long and hard. We'll be at it for years, unless—"

"Unless what?"

"Oh, it's silly. Never mind." He fiddled with a tiny silk banner hanging from the model's battlements.

"Why don't you tell us?" Driskoll asked. "Maybe we can help you."

"Well . . ." The little banner snapped off, and Hadrian rolled it between his fingertips. "What we need is some magic. But I don't know any wizards who are willing to spend their time building a castle."

Kellach puffed up like a bullfrog. "I'm a wizard," he said importantly.

"Apprentice wizard," Driskoll put in.

"What do you need a wizard for?" Moyra asked.

Hadrian's eyes gleamed. "I want to bring the magic back."

"What?"

"There's only a little magic left in the place," Hadrian

answered, "and what's left is all mixed up."

"That explains a few things," Driskoll muttered.

"The place needs a wizard—a young strong, powerful wizard who can put everything right again," Hadrian said. "Someone to bring the magic back."

Driskoll frowned. "That sounds like powerful magic. Are you sure Kellach can—"

"Of course." Kellach kept his eyes on Hadrian. "I can do all kinds of useful magic. Name the task."

"This is my lucky day," Hadrian chortled, sticking the tiny banner back on the battlements. It fell off, but he didn't notice.

"But be here first thing tomorrow morning—near the great entrance. And watch out for the giants. They don't care who they step on."

Then he leaned over, picked up the mess of feathers and wire on the floor, and began repairing his gadget.

"Right, then," Kellach said. "I'll see you tomorrow."

Without looking up from his work, Hadrian waved them off. Kellach raced down the steps while Driskoll sulked behind him.

"So let me get this straight," Moyra said when they reached the clearing outside. "First, a bunch of harpies steals this dagger. They deliver it to someone who throws it at you. And now the mantlehorn come and get it back. And now that they have it, you're in danger."

"I'm not in danger," Kellach insisted. "They're deer. How can a deer hurt me?"

"But Hadrian just said—"

"Hadrian's a batty old man. What does he know?"

74

"He knows a lot about this weird old castle," Moyra said as they emerged out into the courtyard. "And you'd better not call him batty if you're going to be working for him."

"Ah yes." Kellach sighed. "Wonder what people pay to have someone bring back the magic in a castle."

"Great," Driskoll muttered to himself. "While he spends the day casting spells and building castle walls, I'll be losing another layer of skin to the erasing potion."

They picked their way through the ruins toward the wall. The sun was about to set and soon it would be dark.

"We'd better get moving," Kellach said. "Curfew."

Driskoll kicked a stone. "You always get to do everything."

Kellach turned around. "Oh that's right, I'm doing everything while I'm keeping you out of trouble—"

"Hold it, you two hags," Moyra cut in. "There's too much going on here to have any more arguments."

Kellach shot a look at Driskoll.

"And besides," Moyra continued, "I still think you're in danger, Kellach. We still don't know who threw that dagger at you. Do you think it was the old man?"

Kellach laughed. "Him? He could barely remember who he was."

"Well, who was it then?"

"Maybe it was the mantlehorn." Driskoll suggested.

"I think we all know who it was," Kellach said, looking straight at Driskoll.

"I didn't do it!" Driskoll shouted.

"I didn't say it was you," Kellach said coolly.

"No, but you were thinking it," Driskoll said.

Moyra groaned and looked away. She stopped suddenly and put her hand on Driskoll's arm.

"What?" Driskoll looked at her and knew something was wrong. Even in the dim light, he could see that the color had drained from her face. She was staring at something straight ahead of them.

Driskoll followed her gaze and saw an immense, ghostlike figure gliding through the castle ruins.

A cracked glass helmet covered its face, and a glassy breastplate hung from its chest. But its skeletal arms and legs were bare. The armor gleamed in the light of the setting sun.

The mirrored ghost knight cut through the darkening gloom. And it was heading right for them.

CHAPTER

13

"Is this what you saw in the moat?" Moyra whispered.

Driskoll shook his head, but he wasn't sure Moyra saw him because her eyes hadn't left the creature, and neither had his.

The ghost, or whatever it was, appeared to have been a knight. It held up a mirrored shield in one of its bony, clawed hands and called out in a deathly voice that sounded like it came through cobwebs, "Knights of the Silver Dragon, your destruction is near. For the Dagger of Doom tears brothers apart and means death to you."

As the knight spoke, it never stopped its slow death march toward them, and Driskoll could feel a searing heat prickle his skin. With just inches separating them, the knight spoke again, "The Dagger of Doom shall—"

And then the knight was gone.

"The Dagger of Doom shall what?" Driskoll asked, looking around. Everything had disappeared, even the castle wall.

Driskoll glanced around. They were standing in a stone

corridor, at the bottom of some kind of stairwell. The air smelled dank and cold.

"Where are we?" Moyra asked. "What happened?"

But Kellach didn't answer. He looked confused, standing with his arms in the air as if in the middle of casting a spell.

"What did you do that for?" Driskoll shouted at his brother. "He was going to say something about the dagger."

"I was trying to send him away, not us," Kellach said, still staring ahead of him as if the ghost knight were still there.

"Send him where?" Moyra asked again.

From the open doorway at the top of the stairs, Driskoll could see the light of the setting sun. The sun cast a dim circle of light onto the floor. Beyond the circle, there was nothing but pitch-darkness. Something about this place was familiar, thought Driskoll.

Driskoll crept toward the stairwell. He turned around and looked back at his brother and Moyra. It was then that he saw the sign above the arched open door.

"TURN BACK!" it read.

There was only one sign in the whole world like that. And suddenly Driskoll knew exactly where they were.

"Uh, Kellach?" Driskoll began. "Is there any possibility you were trying to send the ghost knight to the entrance of the Dungeons of Doom?"

"The Dungeons of Doom!" Moyra groaned. "How could you do this to us?"

A loud, gurgling laugh answered.

"Kellach," Moyra said between clenched teeth. "Get us out of here! There is some kind of creepy creature down here!"

The laugh snapped through the dank air again as if it came from the deepest, darkest recess of the earth.

"It's coming!" Driskoll said.

Driskoll heard the hushed and quick "thrrrp" of Moyra's knife being drawn, and he pulled out his own sword.

"Relax," Kellach said, the confidence returning to his voice. "Whatever it is, it's just trying to scare us."

Driskoll held his sword in front of him and listened. Everything was silent.

Then a small green creature stepped into the circle of light. Its bald head was abnormally large for a stumpy body. Its dirty, green skin was mottled with large, oozing sores. Two tiny black eyes dotted its face, and between bouts of devilish laughter, it stuck its thumb in a little black hole that Driskoll guessed was its mouth.

"I've got it," he shouted, slashing at it with his sword. "It's right here."

The face disappeared into the darkness, and Driskoll felt a piercing, burning pain in his leg. "Ow! It bit me!"

Driskoll waved his sword, but Kellach stopped him.

"Look," Kellach said, pointing at its tiny, jet black eyes. "It's just a baby ogre. It doesn't even have horns yet."

"I don't care if it's a baby bird! It bit me," Driskoll wailed. "The little—"

"Oh come on," Kellach said. "A baby ogre is pretty harmless—ouch!"

Kellach grabbed his leg and hopped up and down.

The creature bit into Kellach's wizard robes and didn't let go. "Get off!" he yelled, trying to fling it away. But the creature had completely attached itself to the hem of his robes, like a small demon dog.

"All right." Kellach clenched his teeth. "You want to play, Little Ogre Monster? We'll play."

Kellach stopped flailing and stood still. The ogre began chewing on Kellach's robes.

"Give me your knife, Moyra!" Kellach said, snatching it out of her hand. Kellach chanted softly and waved a knife in a circle above his head.

"No, Kellach," Moyra shouted. "You saw what happened with the knight just now." But Kellach ignored her.

The tip of the knife lit up, and soon it burned like a red-hot poker. Kellach dangled the knife in the air over the little attacker.

The ogre caught sight of the fiery knife and let go of Kellach's robes, leaving a trail of spit on the hem. Then Kellach tossed the knife in the air.

The ogre waddled after it as the knife sizzled through the darkness. The light cast from the knife gave an even more sickly green glow to the baby ogre's skin.

"Let's get out of here!" Driskoll cried as he headed for the stairs.

Kellach pulled him back by his jacket. "No, wait. This is going to be good."

The baby batted at the knife, which swung lazily just out of its reach. With every missed attempt, the ogre grew more peevish. Then, just when it looked like it was going to launch into a full tantrum, the knife stopped, and the ogre made contact. It grasped the red-hot knife in its clawed little fingers, with a look of complete triumph on its face.

And just when Driskoll thought it couldn't get any uglier, its face contorted into a look of such extreme agony that Driskoll almost had to turn away.

It ran in circles, still clutching the burning knife.

"Drop it, you idiot!" Driskoll yelled.

Finally, the knife shook slightly, and the ogre released it. It stumbled and tried to stuff its entire fist in its mouth as it fled back into the dark recess of the dungeons. The knife began to follow, but at a word from Kellach, it stopped and fell, smoking, to the ground.

Driskoll could have sworn he heard a giggle coming from the knife as it burned out, but it was probably Moyra standing next to him.

They listened as the ogre's howls died away in the distance. Kellach walked over, picked up Moyra's knife, and handed it back to her.

"See?" he said. "I told you it would be good."

"You're right," Driskoll said, rubbing his leg where the ogre had bitten him. "That was brilliant. Now if only you could have done something like that to that ghost-knight thing—"

"Forget the knight," Moyra said as she headed up the stairs. "Let's go home before that ogre comes back with mommy."

CHAPTER

14

With every step he took on the dark road back to Curston, Driskoll looked around anxiously.

"First there was the creature in the moat," he said. "Then the dagger. And now that ogre. That's the third time someone tried to kill you today, Kellach."

"Don't be ridiculous," Kellach answered without looking back. "The thing in the moat was after all of us. Same with the ogre. It bit you first after all."

"Don't forget about that nasty knight," Moyra added. "Did you notice that his armor was made out of mirrors?"

"It wasn't much of a suit of armor, was it?" Kellach asked. "Looked pretty old and cracked to me."

"You're missing the point," Moyra said. "Hadrian said that Promise Castle was destroyed by the Knight of Mirrors."

"And that guy was . . ."

"The Knight of Mirrors, yeah," Moyra said.

"So now," Driskoll mused, "it isn't just Kellach who's in danger. It's all the Knights of the Silver Dragon."

"That means all three of us," Moyra said nodding.

"Why would anybody want to get rid of us?" Driskoll asked.

Moyra snorted. "Where have you been the last six months, Dris? Seems like someone's been out to get us ever since we became Knights of the Silver Dragon."

"Well, anyway," Kellach said, pointing ahead, "We're almost home."

They could see the everburning torches marking the entrance to the Westgate. Watchers, under the direction of Torin, patrolled the top of the wall day and night, keeping monsters away from the city.

Driskoll knew that Kellach had no magic that could get them past the watchers. But it was late, and he wanted to get home.

"So what do we do now?" he asked. "They won't let us in past curfew."

"We could try the thieves' entrance," Moyra muttered as she dug her hands into her pockets. "But I'd have to blindfold you two, or the thieves guild would kill me." She pulled out a piece of lint and shook her head. "I don't have anything on me that we could use to cover your eyes."

"Forget it," Kellach said as they approached the gate. "We don't need blindfolds. I have a better idea. Watch this."

A huge watcher stuck his head out over the battlements on the top of the wall. He pointed a sharp spear down at the three kids. Driskoll recognized him as one of the largest and meanest of the watchers.

Kellach touched his forehead in a kind of casual salute. "Greetings, Mogurg."

"It's Mobrick," the watcher sneered.

"Oh, sorry, Moburp."

"What are you doing?" Driskoll whispered. He didn't think making a watcher angry was the way to get through the gate.

But Kellach continued walking briskly forward. "We just came from a mission in the ruins, and we're dead tired," he said. "Let us pass."

Mobrick sniggered. "The town is closed for the night. No one gets in after dark. Not even the sons of Torin who call themselves Knights. Go back to the ruins and die."

"Sorry," Kellach said. "I'm too young for that kind of nonsense. Let us pass."

Mobrick aimed his spear at Kellach's heart. "Take a step closer," he growled, "and I'll skewer you."

Kellach sighed. " I tire of this." He pointed at the spear and chanted something. The weapon slid out of the watcher's hands and hung above his head, much the same way Moyra's knife had floated earlier.

An alarm went up, the gate clanked open, and suddenly ten watchers surrounded the kids.

"Great, Mister Brilliant Wizard," Moyra whispered. "Now, what were you planning to do?"

Driskoll looked at the watchers. They were mostly men, and some were unusually large species of elves. They formed a line so thick they could barely be distinguished from the wall itself. Kellach lowered the spear into Mobrick's hands.

"Just checking to make sure you were all on your toes," Kellach said, chuckling.

One of them mumbled something about hanging the little

brat from his toes, and a few of the others snickered.

"Silence," Mobrick thundered. "Little children don't check on watchers—unless they want to learn a lesson." He prodded Kellach with his spear.

Just then a short shadowy figure moved in front of Mobrick.

As he moved into the torchlight, Driskoll could see his face. It was Gwinton. The burly dwarf sheathed his double-edged axe as he caught sight of the two boys.

"Let them pass, Mobrick," Gwinton said. "They're Torin's offspring." He stepped slightly aside, leaving the tiniest open space in the line.

Kellach smiled triumphantly and started walking through the gap. Driskoll and Moyra followed uneasily.

Gwinton nudged Driskoll as he passed. "You were lucky I was here to watch over you," he said. "But don't make the same mistake twice."

Driskoll nodded and hurried to catch up with his brother and Moyra.

As he passed through the gate, something caught Driskoll's eye. There, standing across from the gate, watching everything was the black-haired man from Main Square.

Driskoll stopped and stared. Moyra looked up and gave a slight gasp as she saw him. She grabbed Driskoll and led him to the other side of the gate.

"It's like he was waiting for us," she whispered as they hurried away.

A chill ran up Driskoll's spine. "There's so much going on around here," he said. "Let's go back to the castle and talk to

Hadrian. Maybe he can explain—"

"No way," Kellach said. "You heard that knight—we're all in danger now."

"We're already in danger," Driskoll said. "When Dad hears about the way you talked to the watchers, he'll kill us."

"But he's not going to hear about it, right?" Kellach said. "Or else he'll hear about how you stole the scroll from Oswald."

Driskoll stopped. He clenched his fists and looked away, trying hard to control his anger.

"He's going to hear about it, Kellach," Moyra said wisely. "You know he will. That was Gwinton who let us in back there. The only reason the watchers didn't kill us as soon as you opened your mouth was because Torin's your dad. But Gwinton's probably summoning him right now."

Kellach shrugged.

"Just because you made one teeny mistake with the Knight of Mirrors," Moyra said, "it doesn't mean you have to make up for it every chance you get."

"I didn't make a mistake." Kellach turned quickly on Moyra.

She fell silent, and Driskoll knew it wasn't out of fear. She was just as puzzled about Kellach's behavior as he was.

The three headed in silence down the road.

"I think we should all get some rest right now," Kellach said, glancing at Driskoll. "And don't get any ideas about going back to the castle tonight. I forbid it."

"What?" Driskoll shouted. "You can't do that!"

"You think so?" He raised his hands and stared at Driskoll.

"You think another of your stupid spells is going to scare me?" Driskoll crossed his arms over his chest.

Moyra jumped in between them. "Stop it, both of you. Arguing isn't doing anyone any good."

Driskoll ignored her and stared up at his brother. "You can't talk to me that way . . ."

"I'm going home," Moyra said. "Let me know when you stop fighting."

Kellach ignored her too. He looked at Driskoll. "I can talk to you that way because I'm your older brother. I'm the one who's watching out for you. I'm the wizard."

"Some wizard," Driskoll scoffed. "Can't even make an old knight disappear."

CHAPTER

15

Driskoll and Kellach returned home in silence. Driskoll wasn't surprised that the house was empty. Torin usually worked late into the night and sometimes didn't come home at all.

Kellach crawled into bed without a word. A moment later the sound of soft snores came from under the covers.

But Driskoll couldn't sleep. He tossed and turned on his lumpy bed, his heart racing. He expected his father to bolt in at any moment in a firestorm of anger over what had happened at the gate. Torin would probably confine them to their room for a month.

Actually Driskoll thought that would make a suitable punishment—for Kellach.

Of all the mysteries he'd encountered that day—the dagger with Kellach's name on it, the disappearing castle, the strange deer, the ghostly knight—the most puzzling was Kellach's behavior.

First he had acted boldly stupid at the Westgate. But a few minutes later, he backed down, acting too scared to return to the castle. When was the last time Kellach wanted to get some rest instead of solving a mystery? Driskoll thought.

Suddenly he sat up, remembering the girl, Willeona. Maybe she had put some sort of spell on Kellach.

Driskoll threw off the covers. He might as well do something useful. He tiptoed over to his jacket and pulled out the dagger drawing. At least that was something he could figure out. Staring at it by the light of the moon shining though his window, Driskoll pored over the runes.

He couldn't decipher runes the way Kellach could, but he could read letters. And now that he looked at them, they looked a lot more like letters than runes. He went to his desk and pulled out a piece of parchment, a quill, and a bottle of ink. Dipping the quill in the ink, he copied down the runes exactly.

The first letter didn't look like anything he knew. He doodled on it for a bit, finally drawing a line connecting the three horizontal lines:

E

He sat back and looked at the rest of the letters. The second letter was definitely a V.

"So that gives us EV . . . ," he whispered.

He looked at the third and fourth letters: two I's.

"Evii." Frowning, he looked at the last letter. It almost looked more like an L.

He said the letters aloud.

"E . . . V . . . I . . . L"

He almost knocked the ink bottle over as he said it aloud. "Evil."

The Dagger of Doom said evil on it. What more proof did Driskoll need that the thing was dangerous? Driskoll breathed heavily as he looked at the last five letters.

There was another of those three line letters. He drew a line down it, just as he had done before.

He sounded it out, "Renwo."

"Renwo," he repeated. Could it be another language?

"I bet Hadrian would know more about this," he thought. "He knew about the dagger and the mantlehorn. I'll bet he knows what this means."

He was about to get up and pull on his jacket when he remembered what Kellach had said about not going out tonight.

"Hmmpf," he said, looking at the snoring Kellach. "Who is he to tell me what to do? He acted like a stupid half-orc at the gate tonight."

Driskoll went to the bedroom door and stopped. It would be just like Kellach to put some kind of alarm spell on the door. Or maybe he'd set a magical creature, like an invisible stalker, just outside ready to blast Driskoll as soon as he came out.

He looked around. Kellach was still snoring softly in his bed. Driskoll slowly opened the door and looked into the dark hallway. No alarms blasting, no gongs clanging. And no magical creatures—at least none that he could see, anyway.

He tiptoed downstairs, stealthy as a thief, alert to any sound. Taking a journey into the city at night was always dangerous. He would need a few items from the front closet.

The supply closet was a mass of useful and not so useful items. It was a catchall place for three people living together who had never grown accustomed to cleaning up after themselves. And it was another reminder of his mother's absence.

Jourdain had always kept the closet neat. When Kellach and Driskoll were little, it was a treasure trove of trinkets and treats that could help heal scraped knees and hurt feelings.

Nowadays, when clothes or household items needed repair, they often were dumped in there, mixing with items that their mother had set aside for real emergencies, like extra barrels of water and spare torches. The result was that no one in the household could ever find what he was looking for.

The closet was deceptively large and receded back into a tiny compartment with a secret passageway, which was a protective feature that Torin and Jourdain had designed into their home when it was built.

Thinking of his dad made Driskoll shudder. Torin could come barging in at any moment, and Driskoll was not prepared to deal with the mood his father would be in.

Driskoll rummaged through the closet as quietly as he could. At one point, a small but heavy tin of salt fell on his foot and he started to cry out, but clapped his hand over his mouth.

Eventually he found what he was looking for—a torch and a walking stick. On his way out, he grabbed a length of rope too. You never know, he thought. He closed the door behind him and looked around.

Maybe it had all been needless worry. Kellach was probably trying to scare him, and there were no spells on anything. He chuckled at his own nervousness and put his hand on the front door knob to open it.

It didn't budge.

Dragon dung! Kellach had put a locking spell on the door and no amount of turning or picking at the lock would get Driskoll out.

He tried the back door. Locked. He tried the windows. Locked.

He knew better than to try and force anything, and after the shrieking spell incident that afternoon, he didn't want to deal with any more broken windows that night.

Driskoll looked around. The answers to a lot of mysteries were back at the castle, and he was trapped at home. He wanted to yell and maybe punch something. Sometimes it was so frustrating having a wizard for an older brother.

He looked around hopelessly as he reached into his pocket for the dagger scroll. He remembered when he'd found that business scroll in the back of the closet, and he thought he'd been pretty clever switching the old scroll for this one.

Driskoll stared at the closet, remembering. He had found the scroll near the secret passage.

"The secret passage!" He looked up. "I bet Kellach forgot about it." He opened the closet door again and wedged himself in between the stacks of old clothes and barrels. He had to move a few barrels out of the way, and he collided with several unused mops and brooms. It took a while, but he finally made it to the back of the closet. He felt the floor for the old brass handle. It didn't take long to find.

The trapdoor hadn't been used in years. Driskoll pulled hard.

It inched open just enough to give him some hope. He tugged harder, and the door opened wide. He peered into the passageway. It was narrow and dark, but he was familiar with it. Besides, he had been through enough passages that day.

Driskoll emerged near an apple tree at the back of his house. Climbing out into the foggy night, he felt rather proud of himself. He, an aspiring bard and a younger brother, had outsmarted Kellach, a wizard's apprentice and a pain in the neck.

Now if he could just make it through the city unharmed . . .

Although watchers patrolled the streets, there were reports of people going out for an evening stroll and disappearing forever. Driskoll could hardly forget the hellhounds that had chased him the last time he had broken curfew.

But he put those thoughts out of his mind as he hurried up the path that led to the castle.

Once again, he found himself at the remains of the castle's massive wood door. Driskoll felt a cold chill as he watched the timbers hang like condemned prisoners. He thought of the Knight of Mirrors. How could one knight do all this damage?

From outside the wall, he couldn't see the tower at all. But once he climbed over a pile of rubble and jumped into the open area, he could see it clearly looking tall and proud. A light shone from the topmost window.

Driskoll raced up the circular stone stairway. Hadrian's door was slightly open.

"Hadrian?" Driskoll peeked inside.

Hadrian was sitting at a fireplace, staring at the flames. He jumped when he saw Driskoll. There was nothing in his face that showed he recognized Driskoll.

"It's me, Driskoll," he said. "We met today, remember?"

Hadrian squinted at him. "What in the name of all that is ghostly are you doing out at this hour?" he shouted.

"I'm just trying to find out about the dagger—"

"You should be at home." Hadrian got up and moved toward him. For the first time, Driskoll noticed how tall the old man was.

"But—"

"No buts," he said. "Now go on home. You shouldn't be out late like this. City's full of dangerous creatures. Like those horrible beasts, the mantlehorn. Now go."

Driskoll walked slowly down the steps. Now I've got two mother hens watching over me, Driskoll thought. Kellach and Hadrian.

He headed across the open area and ambled toward the archway. Once again, he had the feeling that someone was watching him. He looked around, but no one was there. As he arrived back at the main door, he thought about the creature in the moat. Could it be the mantlehorn? Could it know something about the dagger? He was itching for more information, and now that he had a torch . . .

"I must be crazy," he thought as he prodded the wooden boards beneath the archway with the walking stick. Nothing happened. He pounded a little harder and the floor began to move. He jumped back as the ground yawned open. Rocks tumbled into the black hole, but now Driskoll remained safely away from it. The opening was about three feet across. Then, just as Kellach had said, the ground began to close up again. Driskoll wedged his stick between the two surfaces and they stopped moving.

Driskoll took a few careful steps forward and examined the opening. He checked his footing. The ground felt solid around him. He lit his torch and lowered it into the hole, but he couldn't see anything.

Tugging slightly at the walking stick, he made sure it would keep the hole open. Then he grabbed the rope and tied it to a nearby boulder. He lowered the rope into the gap and with a deep breath, he jumped.

He landed on the familiar damp ground.

To his left, about five paces away, he could dimly see a mossy stone wall. In front and behind him, there was nothing but blackness. He breathed the familiar, rotting odor and listened carefully for any small sound. He tugged at the rope and took a last look up at the hole in the ceiling to make sure it hadn't closed.

Wisps of fog drifted eerily through the gap, reassuring him. Then just as he bent down to begin his search, he heard the rattling breathing again. This time, though, it was coming from directly in front of him. He drew his sword.

"Who's there?" Driskoll couldn't stop the shaking in his voice. The strained breathing continued, and Driskoll felt something large near him. He tried to lift his torch, but his arm wouldn't move. Why had he come down here? He was alone, facing an unknown monster, probably from the ruins. The breathing grew louder.

Snap.

He looked up and saw that the pressure from the opposing sides of the gap had been too much for the walking stick, and it had broken in two. Driskoll watched helplessly as the floor closed and sealed him into the moat with the creature right in front of him, blocking his only other way out.

And then he realized he'd made another fatal mistake. He had looked up. The creature had taken advantage of his distraction and knocked the torch and the sword out of his hands.

Driskoll tried to stop shaking, but his voice quivered as he called out again.

"Who's there?"

A pair of black beady eyes gleamed directly in front of him. The breathing stopped.

Driskoll searched the ground for the sword and the torch.

He felt something sharp on his hand, and he shrieked in terror.

Something croaked, "Bardman?"

CHAPTER

16

D riskoll's mouth was wide open in a yell, but he couldn't make any sound come out.

The voice croaked again, "Bardman?"

He slowly closed his mouth and opened it again. The smell, the black eyes, the breathing—it all made sense now. "Ruida?"

The harpy croaked again as she eased her viselike grip on his hand. Driskoll heard her pick up something from the ground. She tossed him the torch.

"Uh, what are you doing here, Ruida?" Driskoll tried to sound calm as he grasped the torch in shaking hands. He was afraid to ask the next question, but he had to know. He gulped. "How did you get out of your cage?"

Ruida croaked and coughed. Driskoll guessed it was her way of laughing. "Harpies get out of cages easy," she rasped.

Driskoll remembered dropping food in between the bars of her cage earlier that morning. He'd sat there for nearly half an hour telling her the story of the Dagger of Doom as if she were just another member of an audience and not a birdlike monster who could have let herself out of the cage at any moment and plucked his eyes out.

"Ruida not hurt Bardman. Ruida like stories."

Driskoll was only slightly relieved. But he did wonder how she got there.

"Bardman say he bring meat back. Ruida wait and wait but no Bardman. Bardman seem interested in castle, so Ruida go look for him here." She looked around. "Find nice moat. Just right for Ruida. Fall asleep. Then Bardman and Wizardboy come."

The effort of so many words made her break into a coughing fit again. After she calmed down, she spoke again.

"Bardman not tell Wizardboy that Ruida is here?"

Driskoll smiled a little. He was Bard*man*, but Kellach was Wizard*boy*.

"Sure," he said, feeling a little better.

"Good," Ruida rasped. "Wizardboy too high and mighty."

Driskoll chuckled slightly. For a harpy, she understood a few things. Feeling a bit more relaxed, he tried a question. "Uh, Ruida, I'm trying to find out about that dagger. You said the harpies stole it. Where did they get it?"

"Ah, that good question, Bardman. Harpies get dagger from mountain. Mountain too high for humans to climb. Only harpies can fly high enough to get it."

"Mountain? Do you mean this hill here?"

Ruida chortled. "Bardman think world is as big as Bardman can walk. But harpies fly to ends of world. Four Legs' mountain is far away."

"Four Legs? What's that?"

"Four Legs live on mountain. Guard dagger. Harpies get dagger from Four Legs."

Driskoll stared at her. "And then what did you do with it?"

Ruida croaked feebly, "Ruida hungry and wing hurt. Bardman not bring food." She gave a long, slow croak.

Driskoll ignored her hint. "Tell me what happened after you got the dagger."

"Ha! Ruida tell Bardman story! Ha! But Ruida need food."

"Ruida needs to tell Bardman the story," Driskoll answered sharply for the first time. "Then Bardman will get food for Ruida."

Suddenly there was a loud cry, and Driskoll saw a blaze of blood red wings flapping. He felt something large and sharp close around his throat. Driskoll couldn't breathe.

The old harpy might have been injured, but she could still wrap her sharp talons around his neck and strangle him.

"Bardman can't see Ruida in dark," she said softly. "But Ruida can see Bardman."

Something covered his torch, and the flame went out. Driskoll shuddered.

"All-all right," he stuttered. "I'll find food. And then you can answer some more questions."

"Good Bardman," she chirped, letting go of his throat. "Ruida never forget. Repay Bardman someday."

Driskoll could hear her dragging herself across the floor. She bumped up against a wall, and the planks above them slid open.

"Bardman get out of moat if Bardman know where to look," she croaked.

Driskoll sighed and grasped the rope, hoisting himself out through the hole. The fog still swirled around the gap in the ground, which closed noiselessly.

Driskoll turned and headed for the market. Now he knew he was crazy. He was going to get food for a foul, murderous creature. But Ruida had offered a clue to the dagger. It might be worth it.

The butcher's tent was at the farthest end of the row of stands. Driskoll passed the pen where drowsy sheep stared at the night air. He followed the sound of buzzing flies to an open area just behind the tent and held up his torch to see what was left of the butcher's wares.

At his feet, he saw a swollen lump of day-old rotting meat clinging to a large bone. Even the buzzards had passed it up, but to Ruida, it would be a feast.

Driskoll almost threw up at the smell of the thing. He held his breath, closed his eyes, and slowly bent down. He reached out blindly and touched something furry and moving. It was the swarm of flies that had collected on the meat. He gagged and jumped away.

Four Legs. Knowing that Ruida would give him more information about this newest clue strengthened his resolve. He tried again. This time, he managed to grab hold of the rotting piece of carcass. Holding it as far from him as possible, he headed back for the castle, followed by a trail of flies.

He tried to get his mind off the disgusting piece of foul meat in his hands by trying to sort through all the questions in his head. Who, or what, was Four Legs? Ruida had said that Four Legs guarded the Dagger of Doom. So maybe the harpies had stolen it from this Four Legs and delivered it to the mantlehorn.

He thought about Ruida. How had he and Kellach missed seeing her fly up to the castle? Could it have been the old harpy who had attacked Kellach with the dagger? But that didn't make sense. A harpy wouldn't need a dagger to kill Kellach, even if she didn't like him. She could just sink her talons into him. And besides, the attacker had been fast and silent. Ruida was definitely neither.

Driskoll knew that this Four Legs was a missing piece to the puzzle. As he climbed the path toward the castle, he saw something in the distance. Something gray and ghostly.

"Oh no," he thought. "Not now."

The Knight of Mirrors stood in the clearing. An intense heat radiated from his ghostly armor, as he drew nearer.

Driskoll thought the knight's armor looked a bit shinier, and there was more of it covering his horribly skeletal body.

"Knight of the Silver Dragon," it said in that same deathly voice. "You have saved yourself once. But it shall not happen again. The Dagger of Doom drives brothers apart. It shall be your destruction."

As the knight held up his shield, the heat grew stronger. But Driskoll could not take his eyes off the mirrored shield. He could see his own reflection swirling around in it.

But it wasn't Driskoll anymore. It was his brother.

Kellach looked out at Driskoll, with his normally confident stare replaced by a look of complete fear.

And then, just as soon as it had appeared, Kellach's face disappeared, and another face looked out at Driskoll. A girl. She was rather strange looking with golden eyes and a long nose. She held something in her hands. The Dagger of Doom. It dripped with blood.

The bell of the Cathedral rang out in the distance, and the vision instantly went dark. Driskoll strained his eyes but could see nothing of the vision, the shield, or the knight.

He stared at the spot where the knight had stood. He'd seen that girl before. It was Willeona.

He picked up the meat and walked on wobbly legs to the entrance of the moat. He threw a rock at the planks. They opened slowly, and he stepped back.

"Ruida! I've got your food," he called. "It's time to talk." He stopped and listened. A heavy snore came from below.

"Ruida?" The snoring was louder than her usual breathing. He threw the meat into the hole and ran all the way home.

17

Driskoll awoke early the next morning. He looked at Kellach's bed and saw that Kellach had already left for his first day of work at the castle.

The house was quiet, and Driskoll knew no one was home. He wondered if his dad had returned at all last night and if he had heard about Kellach's antics at the gate. He shuddered to think about his father's reaction, but he was more worried about the vision he had seen in the Knight of Mirrors' shield.

First Kellach had looked deathly afraid. Then Willeona had been holding the blood-drenched dagger. It couldn't have been any clearer: Willeona was going to try to kill Kellach with the dagger.

Driskoll headed over to Oswald's. If he finished his scroll-tending work quickly enough, maybe he could go up to the castle and tell Kellach about it.

Of course Kellach would be angry when he found out that Driskoll had sneaked out the night before. But once he knew the truth about Willeona and the dagger, he would be thanking Driskoll for warning him.

But when Driskoll arrived at the bard's house, he heard wailing coming from the bedroom. He hurried in and saw the cleric Latislav by the window, preparing a potion in a little cauldron.

Oswald was lying in his bed, the covers pulled up around his face. "Ah, he is finally here," he moaned. "Latislav, do you see how he abandons me at my hour of death?"

"It's a good thing I came to deliver manuscripts for erasing," Latislav murmured, shooting a frosty look at Driskoll. "Or he would be dead by now. There is no one else in the city who can prepare an antidote."

Oswald wailed loudly, "You see, good Latislav? I knew he would kill me before the summer is over."

"What happened?" Driskoll asked.

"A lot you care," the bard shrieked. "I lie here, wasting away, hungry, and forgotten——"

Latislav cleared his throat. "The bard has been poisoned," he said calmly. He held up the empty bottle of celestial mead and glared at Driskoll. "Where did this come from?"

Driskoll stared at the bottle. "A stranger brought it."

"A stranger?" The cleric raised an eyebrow. "What did he look like?"

"Er, I'm not sure if it was a he or a she. I couldn't see a face."

The cleric put the bottle down and returned to the cauldron. "And I suppose you have no idea who this stranger was." He scooped some of the liquid out of the cauldron with a ladle and poured it carefully into a teacup. Then he carried it to Oswald's bed.

"No," Driskoll said. "The person had a brown cloak on. I couldn't see anything."

Oswald was eyeing the vial of bubbling brown liquid. "Eh," he said, "perhaps I could have something else. Some nice vegetable soup for example?"

"Now, now Oswald," Latislav said. "You've already had some of the antidote this morning, and you were fine. Of course you were unconscious at the time."

Oswald peeked up at the cleric. "Could I possibly have something to nibble on with this?" he pleaded. "A bite of cheese? Some potato? A small meat pie?"

The cleric forced a teaspoonful of potion into Oswald's mouth. He gagged and swallowed it loudly.

Driskoll started backing toward the door. "So I guess there won't be any scrolls for me to clean today . . ."

Oswald wailed again "Do you see how he abandons me in my hour of suffering, Latislav? Oh, what is a poor, starving bard like me to do?"

"You are to take your medicine," Latislav said. "The boy is not needed here now while you sleep."

Latislav looked back at Driskoll. "But I would like to know more about this stranger. Did anyone else see him?"

"Oswald did," Driskoll said. "He talked to him at the door."

"Yes," Latislav said. "He might have. But it is unfortunate that Oswald has lost his memory of the last two days."

Oswald had finished his potion. "Not bad." He shrugged. He pointed at Driskoll. "The boy did it. I am sure of it, Latislav." Then he shut his eyes and fell asleep with the teacup still in his hands.

"I do not believe," Latislav said, looking sternly at Driskoll, "that a boy your age could get his hands on a poison such as this. Only a master wizard could create a deadly potion so powerful yet nearly impossible to detect."

He looked at the bottle again. "If you see this stranger in the brown cloak again, you must tell me or your father immediately."

Driskoll nodded and the cleric studied him shrewdly. "There is no work here for you today. You may leave."

Driskoll bolted for the door and headed toward the castle.

Oswald poisoned? Who would want boring Old Oswald dead? And why?

Driskoll was mulling over everything when a hand suddenly clasped his shoulder.

He jumped and turned around. It was Moyra.

"Don't sneak up on me like that."

Moyra laughed. "So is Old Oswald asleep again today?"

Driskoll explained what had just happened at the bard's house.

"But why would anyone want to poison the old bard?" Moyra asked.

"I'm not sure, but I think it has something to do with the dagger," Driskoll said. "Oswald told the stranger who gave him the bottle of poison that the scroll had been erased."

"But you said yourself that he might have been talking about some other scroll."

"I know, but it's not looking that way anymore. That scroll had the Dagger of Doom on it. We know the dagger is dangerous. Someone doesn't want it around."

Moyra looked at him. "You've still got that scroll, haven't you?"

Driskoll touched his jacket uncomfortably.

"You've got to get rid of that thing, Driskoll. It's bad."

"It's not as dangerous as the real dagger," he said. "And I'm going to get the real dagger back."

"As long as that stranger doesn't get you first," she said.

CHAPTER

18

Kellach met them halfway up the path to the castle.

"So, has your dad heard about last night yet?" Moyra asked.

Kellach scowled, but Driskoll didn't pay attention.

"Kellach, I've got something to tell you," Driskoll said.

"And I've got something to show you," Kellach said. "But not now, little brother. I've got to get back to Hadrian. If you haven't noticed, this place is a madhouse."

Driskoll looked around. The path was jammed with people Driskoll had never seen before. There were large burly men swinging pickaxes and thickset dwarves carrying mysterious-looking toolboxes. Families of elves and humans seemed to scatter about in confusion, and there were several parents searching for lost children.

A fat elf pushing a handcart nearly rammed into Driskoll. "Watch where you're going, you ugly brute," the elf shouted over his shoulder.

"Castle builders, " Kellach snorted. "Hadrian says they've

come from the far corners of the earth. And they're not the most polite people you'll meet."

"I'll say," Driskoll grumped as the elf disappeared into the crowd.

"Come on," Kellach said. "I think Hadrian is over here." The kids followed Kellach along the path that led around the castle's crumbled wall. When they came to a clearing in the forest just below the wall, they found Hadrian in the center of an angry crowd. Hadrian was shouting at three huge men at once. None of them spoke the same language, but Hadrian didn't seem to notice. He was red in the face and waving his arms angrily.

Driskoll heard the sound of hooves beating the earth. He turned and saw a horse and rider picking their way through the crowd. Oh no, he thought.

He didn't need to look beyond the horse's official regalia to know who the rider was.

Torin.

But he wasn't looking at the kids. In fact, Driskoll was relieved to see that Torin hadn't even noticed them. Instead, he had his hawk eyes fixed on Hadrian.

As Torin rode up, many of the people who had been arguing fell silent and made a respectful clearing. Even these newcomers could sense that Torin was someone you didn't cross. Only Hadrian hadn't noticed him. He was still shouting and waving his arms, although no one responded. Everyone was staring at Torin.

"I presume you are in charge here?" Torin rumbled.

Hadrian stopped and glanced up. "Yep, I'm in charge," he grumbled. "And I'm not hiring workers. You need to see Scraper about that."

Driskoll moved deeper into the crowd, hiding behind a woman carrying a sleeping baby.

Torin stared coldly at Hadrian. "Do you have a building permit?"

Hadrian scratched his head and peered up at the rider. "Oh, you must be the captain of the watch. Where have you been?" he groused. "I need you to keep order around here."

Torin's eyes flashed, but he didn't move. "I asked if you have a building permit."

"A what?"

"A. Building. Permit." Torin's eyes bored into the old man.

"Oh yes, let's see." Hadrian put his hands on his hips and looked around the crowd as if someone else might have such a thing. He looked back up at Torin. "I can't remember."

Even from several paces away, Driskoll could see a vein throbbing in Torin's left temple. He knew that vein. It throbbed the same way whenever Torin was angry with Driskoll.

"Construction in this city requires approval and a building permit." Torin took his dark eyes off Hadrian and gazed at the castle wall behind him. "Otherwise, this is an unlawful assembly, and you will be fined." He glared at Hadrian again. "And sent to jail."

A murmur went through the crowd as Hadrian looked vaguely at Torin. "Building permit," he muttered, rummaging around his massive apron pockets.

"Is this it?" He retrieved a crumpled scroll and brandished it in front of Torin.

Torin snatched the wrinkled parchment and made a point of smoothing it out with his hands. He studied it for a moment.

"Very well." He handed the scroll back to Hadrian. "You have until evening to bring order to this place."

He steered his horse around and began moving off as Driskoll let out a deep breath.

"Thank you kindly," Hadrian called after him. "I'm sure your son will help keep order."

Now Driskoll froze as Torin stopped his horse and turned around. "What did you say?"

"I said your son will help me keep order," Hadrian piped cheerfully. "He's a wizard, isn't he? The other boy and the girl can help him."

"Where are they?" Torin said in a low voice, his eyes scanning the crowd.

Driskoll wished he were standing under the archway again. Being swallowed up by the moat would be better than dealing with his father there.

"There they are," Hadrian shouted, pointing directly at Driskoll. "You there, young ruffians. Come out and show your father how useful you are."

Everyone turned, including the woman with the baby. Driskoll could barely move, but Kellach came out of nowhere and tugged at his arm. They stepped forward, with Moyra behind them. Driskoll glanced quickly at his father. He had never seen Torin's face quite so purple.

Torin dismounted and pointed to the ground in front of him. The kids dragged themselves over and stopped short in front of Torin. He towered over all of them. Out of the corner of his eye, Driskoll could see Hadrian doing a little jig. The old man had no idea how much trouble the kids were in.

"Why aren't you at the bard's?" Torin asked Driskoll.

"Oswald's sick," Driskoll squeaked. "He—"

Torin didn't let him finish. "A building site is no place for children," he growled. "Return home immediately."

"We're not children," Kellach said.

Someone in the crowd coughed uncomfortably. A few people pretended not to see, but most leaned closer to listen.

"We've been in much more dangerous situations than this."

It was the wrong thing for Kellach to say. Torin's eyes narrowed even further. "Yes, and I hear you made quite a dangerous situation for yourselves at the Westgate last night."

Kellach looked at the ground.

"What were you thinking?" Torin continued. "Baiting my watchers like that? You put the whole city in danger!"

Kellach spoke without looking up, "I was just—"

"You were showing off. I'll not have any son of mine using his position to get a free pass at the gate after curfew. The watchers should have kept you outside. I cannot begin to imagine a punishment strong enough for this . . ."

From past experience, Driskoll knew that Torin was just getting started. But a large, black-gloved hand grasped Torin's shoulder.

"Excuse me," a deep voice growled.

Torin stopped and closed his eyes, as if silently counting to ten to keep calm. Without looking at whoever had done it, he removed the hand from his shoulder and turned.

If Driskoll had actually been breathing, he would have gasped when he saw that the hand belonged to a tall black-haired man dressed completely in black. But Driskoll had been holding his breath. And now he thought he might faint.

"I might be able to help," the black-haired man said.

Torin looked like he was going to pounce on someone.

"Ah, Scraper." Hadrian bounded up to him. "Glad you're here, young man."

But the black-haired man's eyes hadn't left Torin. "I am Scraper. I'm a master mason, and I am in charge here." He gave Driskoll a quick, sneering look. "It's my job to find slaves—I mean workers—to help with building."

He looked back at Torin. "I heard you giving these three a good tongue lashing. If you're looking for a strong punishment, perhaps I can help."

Torin stared at him. There were very few people who could make him speechless.

Scraper continued, "It is a construction site custom for parents to send wayward children to me. After a few days of cutting stone and laying bricks, children are much more obedient."

Driskoll could see Torin sizing up Scraper.

A watcher ran up.

"Captain, sir," the elf panted. "The Westgate . . . trouble, sir . . . more workers coming in . . . we can't keep order."

Torin waved his hand impatiently. "Assign more men from the Hall. I'll be there in a moment."

The watcher pressed him. "Sir, there are some strange creatures . . . it is mayhem."

Torin looked quickly at Scraper.

"You'll keep your eye on these three?"

"Yes," Scraper said, showing his sharp teeth in a nasty smile. "I will keep them in line."

Torin hesitated. Problems at the gates always took precedence, and Driskoll could see that his father was coming to a decision. And Driskoll knew he wasn't going to like it.

"All right," Torin said, getting on his horse. "See that they work hard." He gave Kellach and Driskoll one last fiery glance and was gone in a cloud of hooves and dust.

Driskoll watched in silence as his father rode away. He would have chosen Torin's punishment—whatever it was—over whatever this Scraper had to deal out.

Kellach tapped on Scraper's shoulder. "I'm supposed to be doing magic. With Hadrian." He pointed at the old man, who seemed to have forgotten what he was doing and was shouting at no one in particular.

Scraper ignored him. Instead he reached into his pocket and drew out a tiny hammer and a small golden disc. Driskoll stopped breathing again and wondered if this instrument had something to do with his punishment.

Scraper glanced at the unruly crowd around him and held the disc up. It had a curious shimmer to it, lit by the morning sun.

Scraper took the hammer and touched it to the disc. Instantly a loud gong rolled through the air like a tidal wave.

Driskoll held his hands to his ears. The sound went right through him and seemed to fill up every part of his body. His head hurt, and his hands and feet were shaking. He looked at the crowd. Incredibly, no one was fainting or running around as if they had just gone deaf. Everyone simply stopped talking and looked at Scraper.

"Much better," Scraper said, and Driskoll was relieved that he had not gone deaf. "You all know what you are here for," he continued in a booming voice. "Carpenters, go to the main door of the castle. Stoneworkers, to the rear of the castle wall."

He paused as Hadrian whispered something in his ear.

"Under no circumstances is anyone to enter the castle grounds within the walls. For now, we are working on the wall and the door only."

Someone raised a hand to ask a question, but Scraper continued.

"Payment is at the end of the week as usual. I do not need to remind you all that I do not like disorder."

With that, he put away the gong, and the crowd began breaking up. To Driskoll's utter amazement, everyone began moving about in an orderly fashion. Some of them picked up their carts and bustled away, while others began stacking stones into neat piles. Everyone looked like they knew what to do.

Scraper stood silent as a gargoyle, watching everything. Then he turned to Hadrian, who had also fallen silent. "It's agreed these children are working for slave wages."

Hadrian nodded. "You can have those two, but I've got this one." He pointed at Kellach as if he were a piece of timber.

Kellach grinned.

"Figures," Driskoll whispered to Moyra. "Kellach will hardly lift a finger while we break our backs. And it's all his fault we're in this mess."

Scraper cracked his gloved knuckles and sneered at Driskoll. "Do not try to leave. I will know if you do. And I do not like slaves who escape."

CHAPTER

19

Kellach tapped Driskoll on the shoulder. Keeping his back to Hadrian and Scraper, he reached into his robes and pulled something shiny out.

The blade was hidden in a sheath, but Driskoll recognized the handle of the Dagger of Doom.

"How—where—?" Driskoll stuttered.

Kellach chuckled. "Willeona found it," he said.

Driskoll was so angry he couldn't speak. He wasn't even sure he wanted to tell Kellach how dangerous it was.

"You should put that thing away," Moyra whispered, looking around at the crowd. "I don't trust any of these people."

Suddenly Scraper stormed up. His eyes traveled to the dagger in Kellach's hands and he glared at Kellach. Driskoll held his breath, waiting for Scraper to do something to Kellach. But he just stared at the dagger in Kellach's hand.

Hadrian walked up and stopped when he saw the dagger.

"Ah," he said, "now we'll get some serious work done on this castle. Come along, boy." He pulled Kellach away.

Scraper remained rooted to the spot, staring at Hadrian and Kellach as they walked toward the opening in the wall and went inside.

Then Scraper looked at Driskoll. "Well, what are you waiting for," he snarled. "Get a move on." He stormed away, beckoning them to follow him.

Driskoll and Moyra sulked after him

"This is not going to be fun," Moyra moaned.

"Yeah, and it's all Kellach's fault. He acted like a stupid troll last night, but we're the ones who have to do slave labor."

"And isn't it convenient that Willeona found that dagger for him?" Moyra said.

"I worked so hard to find that dagger," Driskoll groused. "And he comes sailing up with it in his robes." He mimicked Kellach's sauntering steps. "I don't even want to tell Kellach about the dagger now."

"Tell him what?"

But Driskoll didn't answer. The ground had started to shake, and they both leaned against the castle wall to keep from being thrown backward.

Driskoll looked up. Two stone mountains were walking toward him.

"Stone giants," Moyra whispered as they flattened themselves against the wall so the creatures could pass. It took Driskoll a few minutes before he realized that they weren't actually mountains. But their square, gray faces and massive bodies made them look like they were carved out of marble. Each one carried a rock the size of a horse. The giants trudged forward, oblivious to the humans running around at their feet.

Scraper came up and dragged Driskoll away from the wall. "Come on," he snarled. "I don't like dawdlers."

Driskoll and Moyra scurried after Scraper, who seemed to glide through the crowd like a black bat. They finally caught up with him in a large open area at the back of the castle wall. Several dwarves stood along the wall.

The giants stopped and hurled the stones on the ground, breaking them into smaller pieces. They laughed heartily and walked away.

Scraper pulled some scrolls and a metal ruler out of his bag. A stocky, bearded dwarf carrying a small chisel emerged and followed Scraper as he walked among the rock pieces left by the giants.

Scraper appeared to know the dwarf, but he barely looked at him. He measured each of the stones and muttered to the dwarf, who chiseled fine, straight lines into each of the stones.

When Scraper had measured all of the stones, he raised his hand in the air, and the dwarves who stood along the wall swarmed over the stones. Suddenly chips of rock were flying as the dwarves cut, hammered, and chiseled.

"Pure limestone," one of them called out. "That'll make a good solid wall."

"Better than the one that's there now," another called out, tossing a rock against the wall and watching it sail back. "No dwarf made that."

Scraper didn't comment, but rolled up his scrolls. He looked at Driskoll and Moyra. "Get to work," he growled.

Driskoll and Moyra stared at him. "We're supposed to cut these?" Moyra asked as a small stone chip sailed past her face.

Scraper looked at the dwarf. "Gwynrid, get them some tools," he said. Then he was gone.

The dwarf handed each of them a wooden mallet and a flat iron tool about the size of a knife.

Moyra and Driskoll stared at the dwarf.

"You haven't worked with stone before, have you?" The dwarf sighed.

They shook their heads, and the dwarf rolled his eyes. "Humans," he grumbled. "Can cut wood all right, but don't ask them to do stonework. Oh no. Rocks are too hard, they say."

He grabbed the tools from Driskoll and motioned them over to a large rock. He pointed at the lines he had carved into it.

"You must cut the rock to these lines," he said. "Make your edges neat and clean." He took the iron tool in his fist and laid it against the stone at an angle. Then he whacked at it with the mallet.

"Fang-of-the-vampire!" Moyra flinched. "How are we supposed to do that?"

In about fifteen minutes, the dwarf had chiseled the jagged stone into a perfect rectangular cube. Then he took another smaller iron tool and began scraping the edges to smooth it out. When the dwarf was finished, he took a T-shaped ruler out of his bag.

"The angels must be exact," he said, expertly fitting the T onto the edges. Then he returned the tools to Driskoll. "Now you," he said.

Driskoll marched over to a stone boulder and studied it for a moment. He took the mallet and held the iron bar up to the stone, just as the dwarf Gwynrid had done. He struck the iron bar and the stone exploded, chips of rock flying everywhere. Some of the dwarves exchanged glances.

Gwynrid sighed and took him over to another rock. He stood behind Driskoll, guiding his hand. Slowly, Driskoll chipped away at the stone. He started to feel a rhythm to the steady *chink, chink* of the iron tool against the stone.

A gray-haired female dwarf set Moyra to work on a stone nearby. Driskoll glanced up and could see the concentration in Moyra's face as she chipped away at the rock.

As the cool morning air gave way to the hot afternoon sun, beads of sweat trickled down Driskoll's neck. But slowly, very slowly, he began to make headway into the stone.

Every so often the ground shook beneath him, and the dwarves scattered to the castle wall. Then the giants stomped into the open area and hurled more large stones at the ground.

Scraper then appeared out of nowhere to measure the new stones, while the dwarves remained silent along the wall.

As soon as he was gone, the dwarves went back to work. One of them would strike up a song in the dwarf language, and sometimes the other dwarves joined in.

Driskoll found himself swinging his mallet to the rhythm of the dwarves' deep, rough voices. He felt like he could get lost forever in their haunting music, even though he had no idea what they were singing about.

It took Driskoll nearly five hours to get his stone into a rough rectangular shape, following the line that Gwynrid had made, but he felt a surge of pride as the dwarf patted the stone.

"Good work, for a human," the dwarf said heartily. "After break, we'll show you how to smooth it out."

At that moment, Driskoll heard the loud gong from Scraper's bell, although it was much farther off now, and he imagined Scraper was in some other part of the castle grounds. The dwarves stopped working and retreated to the wall, reaching into their sacks for food.

Driskoll and Moyra stared hungrily at them.

Gwynrid glanced at them and motioned to the gray-haired dwarf who had helped Moyra. She looked at the kids and whispered something to a young dwarf next to her. The teenager got up and approached them. He was slender for a dwarf, but he had typical dwarf features: black hair, tanned skin, and bright green eyes. Driskoll had seen him working on stone and guessed that he was his own age, but the young dwarf had carved seven stones in the time that it had taken Driskoll to cut away at one.

He presented Driskoll and Moyra with two loaves of bread.

"Thank you," Moyra said. The dwarf nodded and went back to the wall.

Moyra held the loaf in her hand. "Why do I have an urge to cut this perfectly straight?" she asked.

Driskoll laughed. This slave labor was hard, but the dwarves weren't scary like Scraper. In fact, he liked working with them.

Driskoll and Moyra slumped against the stone. Driskoll was so tired he wasn't sure if he would be able to chew the bread. Every muscle and bone in his back and neck ached, and his hands were covered in blisters.

"So help me, Kellach," he said aloud.

"So help you what?" Moyra rubbed her neck and looked over at him.

"I don't know," Driskoll said. "It's just not fair. We break our backs all day because of something he did. And he's not even getting punished."

"Hmmpf." Moyra smirked. "I wouldn't be wishing any punishment on him. He's got enough trouble with that dagger."

They both stared at the stones in front of them as they ate their bread in silence. It had taken them nearly all day, but they had finally formed two large rectangular blocks with straight edges.

"So what were you going to tell Kellach?" Moyra asked after they had finished their bread.

Driskoll looked at the dwarves and lowered his voice. "Remember how you said there was something strange about that girl, Willeona?"

Moyra sat up straight. "Yeah," she said. "I've been thinking about her a lot. Don't you think it's weird that she just appeared out of nowhere? I know a lot of people in Curston, but I've never seen her before."

Driskoll nodded. "I saw her last night. The Knight of Mirrors showed me another vision, and she was in it."

"You went out last night?" Moyra fumed, punching him hard on the shoulder. "Don't you care that the Knight of Mirrors told us we were all going to die?"

"Don't you care that your punches could kill me?" Driskoll rubbed his arm.

Moyra swore softly, "You shouldn't have gone out. It's not safe right now."

"Well, I did, and there's nothing I can do about it now."

"All right." Moyra sighed. "Tell me what happened."

Driskoll recounted his late night journey to the castle and how Hadrian had sent him home.

"Yeah well, the old man was right," Moyra put in.

"All right, all right," Driskoll said. "Just let me finish." He explained what Ruida had said about the mountain and Four Legs. Then he told her about the knight and the vision. "First I saw Kellach. Then I saw that girl—Willeona. She was holding the dagger, and it was dripping blood."

Moyra frowned. "So what do you think that means?"

"I have a pretty good idea," he said, reaching for the scroll in his pocket. "I also figured out what the runes on the dagger say. "

Moyra grabbed his arm. "Don't touch that scroll," she hissed. "If someone sees you with it . . ."

"All right," he said, putting it away. "But don't you want to know what it says?" Moyra shrugged as he took the silver tool and drew the letters in the dirt.

"Evil," Moyra read. "Evil . . . Renwo?"

"Yeah, I can't figure out the Renwo part. I think it's some other language."

Scraper's gong sounded again from somewhere in the distance. Their break was over. Driskoll glanced up at the sun. It was only a little while longer until curfew. And then they would be free to go.

He leaned over his stone and began smoothing out the edges with his mallet.

Gwynrid walked up. "So how do you humans like stonecutting?"

"It's hard work," Driskoll said, getting up. "But it's good."

The dwarf nodded. "Not as easy as cutting wood, eh?"

Gwynrid seemed to think that was a funny joke and laughed. "Humans cutting stone." He chuckled. "Better they cut wood."

Driskoll stared at Gwynrid as he walked away. Then he looked at Moyra. "What in the name of St. Cuthbert is he talking about?"

But Moyra grabbed his arm. Her eyes were wide.

"Wood," she said breathlessly. "Ren-wood."

"What are you talking about?"

"Renwo. Renwood. Doesn't that name sound familiar to you?" "Yeah, but from where?"

"Don't you remember when we met Willeona? Kellach introduced her as Willeona Renwood."

Driskoll blinked. Evil Renwo. Evil Renwood.

CHAPTER

20

"Gods!" Driskoll whirled around, dropping his mallet on the ground. "That proves it! Willeona is going to kill Kellach! We have to tell him."

Moyra leaned over and picked up the tool, setting it back in Driskoll's hand. "Hold on, Dris. This doesn't prove anything. You can't go around accusing Willeona of trying to kill anyone until we have some real evidence. We'll just have to ask Kellach more about her when we see him."

"Ask me what?" Kellach came from behind a boulder.

"Where have you been all day?" Moyra asked, wiping her brow.

"The only place a wizard should be," he said. He glanced around at the stonecutters' area. "What are you two doing?"

Moyra pointed proudly at the stones, and Kellach gave them a blank look. "What?"

"We cut them."

"Oh," he said, unimpressed. "That's interesting. But if you really want to cut stone, you should see this." Kellach pulled the dagger out of the sheath and walked over to a stone. He gently dragged the dagger across the lines the dwarf had made, and the stone fell cleanly away, forming a perfect rectangle.

Moyra and Driskoll gaped at the stone.

He grinned. "Hadrian showed me. That's how a wizard cuts stone."

"It took us all day to cut those stones," Driskoll moaned. "And you did it in less than a minute."

Kellach shrugged. "What can I say? You were right, Dris. It's got some powerful magic in it. All you do is touch a stone and it cuts it. Hadrian knows all about it."

The dwarves gathered around Kellach and stared at the dagger.

"What kind of devil blade is this that can cut through stone as if it were butter?" Gwynrid thundered.

"You probably shouldn't be showing off that thing," Moyra whispered.

"Oh come on," Kellach said, picking up a small rock and setting the dagger to it. He quickly carved a small statue of the dwarf out of the stone.

Gwynrid stared at the dagger. "The mirrored Dagger of Doom," he gasped. "It has slain an innocent knight and has no place among honest stonecutters."

Driskoll could see Kellach's surprised reflection in the dagger as he looked at Gwynrid.

He looked at Moyra and Driskoll, but a shadow fell over them as a deep voice behind them boomed.

"Give me that dagger, boy."

Kellach turned and faced Scraper, who wasn't looking at

him, but was staring hard at the dagger.

"It's the Dagger of Doom," Gwynrid shouted. "Get it out of here."

"Give it to me," Scraper said, his eyes boring into Kellach.

Kellach shook his head. "It's mine," he said. "No one touches it."

Scraper took a step closer to him. "And you are on my building site," he said, poking Kellach in the chest. "Disturbing my workers."

"Hey!" Moyra shouted, jumping between Kellach and Scraper. "You can't bully him like that."

Kellach quietly put the dagger back into its sheath and slipped it into his robes.

Scraper's eyes narrowed. "If you don't wish to give me the dagger, you will leave." He gestured to Moyra and Driskoll. "And take your friends with you. I'll not have this kind of disobedience on my site!"

"Come on," Kellach said. "It's nearly the end of the day anyway. Let's go home."

He pushed Moyra and Driskoll toward the path. Driskoll could feel Scraper staring at them as they walked away.

"Kellach," Driskoll said as they walked. "I have something to tell you."

"I can see another argument coming," Moyra broke in. "This is where I get out of here." She ran ahead of them down the path.

In the distance, they heard Scraper's gong ringing, signaling the end of the day. Workers began to stream down the path.

Kellach gripped Driskoll's jacket and pulled him aside. "Okay," he said. "What's so important that you have to tell me?"

Driskoll cleared his throat and began to explain the events of the night before. Kellach listened quietly as they walked until Driskoll got to the part about getting out of the house.

"You went out last night?" he said. "But I had all the doors and windows charmed so they were locked."

"Well, you forgot one," Driskoll said. "The secret passage in the back of the supply closet. The one we used to play in when we were little."

"I specifically ordered you not to go out, and you did anyway," Kellach said.

"Since when do you give me orders?"

"Since you started doing stupid things," Kellach shouted. "Which is pretty much since you were born."

"Look who's talking. Who got us all in trouble at the gate last night?"

"Well, we wouldn't even have been in the ruins if you hadn't led us to this place. Willeona said I need to watch you. She's right. I have to watch you all the time."

Driskoll stared at him. "Willeona's not your friend, Kellach," he said calmly.

"Oh yeah?"

They had reached the main entrance to the castle where they had fallen into the moat the day before.

The workers had all left, and the place was deserted. At first, Driskoll saw the shadow only out of the corner of his eye. He turned. There, again, was the ghostly Knight of Mirrors, standing next to him.

Driskoll could feel his own temperature rising as he remembered all of Kellach's antics over the last few days. The butterflies in his hair, the shrieking curse, the foolishness at the Westgate, and now this. His heart pounded, and he could feel the blood rushing to his head and his eyes until he could hardly see Kellach anymore. All he could see was a red haze. And all he could feel was pure rage.

"Why won't you ever listen to me? Willeona's not your friend. She's trying to kill you!" And then he didn't know why, but the thought came into his head. "She's a beast."

Driskoll didn't know where that came from. But right now he wanted more than anything to hurt Kellach.

"Take it back," Kellach said quietly, moving closer.

Driskoll could feel the Knight next to him, strong and horribly hot. He suddenly felt bigger than Kellach, and far more powerful. He thrust his face forward.

"She's a beast," he repeated, slowly and clearly. Driskoll turned to the knight. There was something triumphant about the knight suddenly. His armor was completely repaired and shining. None of his horrible body was visible now.

Without knowing why, Driskoll drew his sword.

Kellach drew back in disbelief. But he pulled out the dagger and brandished it in front of Driskoll.

But suddenly, everything seemed to slow down. Kellach seemed to be caught in a reddish haze.

A brown animal appeared out of nowhere, and Driskoll slowly realized it was the deer from the other day. Before he could move out of the way, the animal bumped up against him, knocking Driskoll to the ground. His sword flew out of his hands.

The deer stood over Driskoll. He had never seen a creature so angry. Its golden eyes were blazing and its nostrils were flaring. He could almost smell its anger, and Driskoll thought for a moment that it would stomp on him, but it moved away, still staring at him with its blazing golden eyes

Then everything began returning to normal. He sat up. The blurred haze around Kellach disappeared, and the deer bolted away.

Driskoll's temperature was dropping, and he couldn't see the red anymore. The knight was gone too.

The only one still there was Kellach, his hand outstretched, the dagger pointing at Driskoll.

Driskoll looked down and saw his own sword lying at his feet. He looked up at Kellach.

"Good-bye," Kellach said quietly. He turned and walked down the hill.

CHAPTER

21

Driskoll walked slowly home, thinking about the Knight of Mirrors and the feeling of power he'd had as the Knight stood next to him.

Driskoll didn't feel powerful now. He just felt stupid.

Kellach wasn't at home when Driskoll got there. He went up to his room and lay on his bed in the dark, staring out the window.

What had happened? He had called Willeona a beast, and he had no idea why. He had threatened his own brother, and even pulled out his sword. What would have happened next if the deer hadn't rammed into him? He thought about the creature. There was something familiar about those blazing eyes. He sat up when he remembered.

Willeona. The eyes were the same.

Of course. The mantlehorn can change from human to deer any time they want.

He looked out the window. So where did this new information get him? If Willeona was a mantlehorn, it only linked her more strongly to the Dagger of Doom.

Driskoll sighed. Every time he figured something out, it pointed to more trouble for Kellach.

"But Kellach won't listen," he muttered, lying back on his bed. "He doesn't want to hear anything I have to say right now."

It was well past curfew when Driskoll heard his brother come in the front door. He strained his ears to listen as he heard the click of a lock.

Click. Click. Click.

Driskoll guessed Kellach was doing a locking spell on each of the doors and windows downstairs.

A few minutes later, Kellach opened the door of their room. Driskoll could see him facing the window.

Click. Locked.

There was so much that Driskoll wanted to tell Kellach, but he couldn't bring himself to say anything. He pretended to be asleep as he watched Kellach quietly hide the dagger under a loose floorboard.

I should say something, Driskoll thought as Kellach climbed into his own bed. Anything. All the things he had wanted to say to Kellach over the long hours of waiting for him suddenly seemed feeble and phony.

And, well, there was the news about Willeona being a mantlehorn, and he was sure Kellach didn't want to hear that.

Driskoll lay in bed worrying about what to do. His eyelids felt heavy. And before long he fell asleep.

■ ▮ ▮ ▮ ▮

Driskoll woke up in a sweat. The room felt hot as if a burning wind had just blown into the room. He was about to throw the blanket off when he heard yelling.

"Nooooo! Driskoll! What are you doing?"

Driskoll shot up out of bed and ran over to Kellach. In the moonlight, Driskoll could see blood in Kellach's bed as Kellach writhed in pain.

"Stay away from me," Kellach yelled. "Get away." He pulled a dagger from his shoulder and pointed it at Driskoll.

"Kellach, it's me, Driskoll. Where'd the dagger come from?" Driskoll shouted.

But Kellach was holding his shoulder and glaring wildly at him. "What did you do?"

"What? I didn't do anything." Driskoll looked wildly at Kellach's shoulder. Blood was seeping though his shirt.

"Don't come any closer," Kellach said.

"Kellach, you're hurt. We have to get help."

"Don't try to deny it, Driskoll. I saw you standing over me," he panted. "You had the Dagger of Doom. You were right there. Don't try to tell me you didn't do it."

"What? I've been asleep this whole time."

"Don't lie to me, Driskoll. You were right here. You threw it at me. Lucky for you, it didn't kill me."

"Kellach, I didn't do it. Don't you think you should lie down?"

But Kellach had gotten up. "In the same room with you? I don't think so." He pulled on his robes and stomped out the door.

Driskoll could only stare in disbelief. How could Kellach have seen Driskoll standing over him? Driskoll had been asleep the whole time. Then he thought about his sword and how he barely remembered taking it out earlier that day.

Driskoll followed Kellach out the door. He had to tell Kellach that he hadn't attacked him with the Dagger of Doom. Or had he?

CHAPTER

22

Driskoll ran down the street after Kellach. He could see him far ahead in the moonlight, clutching his shoulder and running toward the castle. He followed him up the path and to the castle wall.

"Kellach!"

At the sound of Driskoll's voice, Kellach seemed to run faster. He reached the opening in the wall and crawled over the rubble, disappearing into the open area inside.

Driskoll climbed up after him. He could see the crumbling ruins just beyond.

But as soon as he jumped inside the archway, the tower came into full view. A tall figure stood at the open door. It was Hadrian.

Driskoll breathed a sigh of relief at the sight of the old man. Maybe Hadrian would believe him.

Driskoll caught up with them just as Kellach was pulling the dagger out of its sheath.

"Kellach, I didn't do it," Driskoll panted as he nearly collided with Hadrian.

Kellach ignored him. "Here," he said, holding the dagger out for Hadrian. "Can you take this for me? I don't want it anymore."

Hadrian ogled the dagger and looked at Kellach. "You did the right thing by bringing this to me," he said. "This is a dangerous dagger. Got to keep it away from——"

"You've got to believe me," Driskoll blurted. "I would never try to hurt you, Kellach."

Hadrian reached for the dagger, but Kellach whipped around and looked at Driskoll, holding it out of Hadrian's reach. "The house was locked, Driskoll. You were the only one home. I saw you standing there with the dagger."

"Maybe someone was in the house. Maybe someone broke in."

But Driskoll's voice was drowned out by a deafening shriek from above. He looked up. The black sky had turned blood red. It was filled with massive flapping wings and grinning demonic faces.

"Harpies!" Kellach cried. "Get down!"

There were at least twenty of them, and they dived like huge poison spears, sending their horrible stench ahead of them. They slammed into the ground and lay there for a second. But then each one sprang up again, swinging massive bones like clubs and swiping the air with fingernails as long as iron spikes.

They were everywhere, and the best Driskoll could do was to cover his head and duck. His ears were full of murderous shrieking, and he could see nothing but wings and teeth and talons.

He tried to move, but a harpy slammed into him, sending

him flying. Lying in the grass, he desperately hoped Kellach had some kind of strong spell he could work on them.

He spotted a group of harpies dancing around in a circle, like demons around a bonfire. And then he realized that Kellach was in the center, surrounded by them. Kellach jumped and dodged their blows, but they were closing in on him, grinning horribly and screaming in devilish delight.

One of them tried to strike Kellach with her club, but Kellach was too fast for her. He slashed her face with the dagger. She screamed in pain, and all the harpies moved closer.

Driskoll tried to crawl toward Kellach, but something sharp pierced his arm. With a scream, he collapsed on the ground. He writhed in pain as a harpy tramped across his chest, shouting something that sounded like "Deal off! Deal off!"

Driskoll was pinned to the ground. He looked up and saw Kellach still surrounded. A big harpy slammed into Kellach, and he fell hard against another one, slipping down to the ground. With that, all the harpies dived on top of him, and he disappeared beneath them.

"Kellach!" Driskoll shouted, trying to get up. His arm burned with pain.

All he could see was a twisted knot of red bodies.

"Got it!" a harpy screamed. She jumped out of the pile and flew off. The others disentangled themselves and followed, and the harpy that had pinned Driskoll down flew away.

Driskoll looked around. The harpies were gone, but they had left behind a horrible smell. He could see Hadrian, kneeling on all fours just inside the door to the tower. His head was bent low, and he was whimpering loudly.

Out of the corner of his eye, Driskoll could see someone running toward them. It was Scraper. He was flinging rocks at the retreating harpies.

Driskoll dragged himself over to his brother, who was lying face down, very still.

"Kellach," he whispered as he gently turned him over.

The moon shone on Kellach's deathly white and badly cut face. A thick line of blood trickled down his temple. His shoulder was soaked with blood.

He opened his eyes a little. "The dagger is gone," he whispered.

Scraper came up and knelt next to Kellach, reaching into his pocket for a small leather bag. "Harpies," he growled. "What next? This place is doomed."

Scraper examined Kellach's face. He took off his black gloves, reached into his bag, and pulled out two round, glossy leaves, rippled with green and orange. They looked like lily pads with stripes. He put one on Kellach's shoulder and held the other over Kellach's eye.

"Keep them there," he said. Then he looked at Driskoll. "Your arm is cut." He handed him another striped leaf. "Keep that on your arm."

Driskoll took it, and his eyes traveled from the leaf back to Scraper's bare hand. It was gnarled and deeply brown. And there was a strange tattoo on the back of it.

Driskoll's mouth dropped as he saw that it was a dagger. The same dagger tattoo he'd seen on the hand of the stranger who had brought Oswald the bottle of celestial mead. The bottle of mead that had nearly killed Oswald.

138

Scraper had lifted the leaf from Kellach's eye and was peering underneath it. If Scraper had poisoned Oswald, what was he doing to Kellach right now with that weird leaf?

Driskoll stood up. Before he knew what he was doing, he knocked the leaf out of Scraper's hand.

"What are you doing?" Scraper yelled. "Keep that leaf on his eye. Are you trying to kill him?"

The wound above Kellach's eye had started to shrink.

"Yes," Kellach said slowly. "He is trying to kill me."

CHAPTER

23

Scraper looked at Driskoll. "What's he talking about? Are you trying to kill him?"

Driskoll pointed at Scraper. "You're the one trying to kill people! You almost killed Oswald with that poisoned mead."

"Are you cracked?" Scraper said, quickly putting his gloves back on. "Poisoned mead? I don't know what you're talking about."

Kellach got up shakily. The wound on his shoulder and the cut above his eye had both healed thanks to Scraper's magic.

"You, boy, aren't in your right mind," Hadrian said as he staggered up, staring at Driskoll.

Kellach backed slowly down the path, staring at his brother. "Stay away from me."

Driskoll didn't know what to do. He needed to explain to Kellach, but a murderer stood right in front of him. Or at least, someone who had attempted murder.

Driskoll decided that Scraper would have to wait. Right now he needed to talk to Kellach.

He ran after him.

"I told you to stay away from me," Kellach said loudly as Driskoll caught up with him.

"Listen, Kellach. I didn't do anything. I was in my bed the whole time. I've told you that dagger is dangerous. Remember the story, Kellach? Of the two brothers? The brother whose name appears on the dagger is marked for death."

"Yeah, I remember that story," Kellach sneered. "I remember that one of the brothers killed the other one with it."

"But Kellach, I didn't do it." Driskoll hurried to keep up with Kellach as they walked toward the wall. "The dagger, Kellach. It says 'Evil Renwo' on it. Evil Renwo. Evil Renwood. Willeona Renwood?" Driskoll shook his head. "Don't you see? Willeona is a mantlehorn, Kellach. She's behind all of this."

Kellach stopped and stared at him. "Well, you got one thing right, at least," he muttered. "She's a mantlehorn, but she's not evil. And the dagger—well, it's a mirror, Dris. Think about it."

Kellach walked away.

Driskoll stood for a moment staring at Kellach as he walked down the path. Someone came up beside him. He turned and saw Hadrian staring at the night sky.

"Someone should get that dagger back," Hadrian mumbled.

"What? Oh, right. The dagger."

"While those harpies have it, your brother is in trouble."

Driskoll was silent for a moment. "But the harpies probably took it back to the ruins. How would anyone find it?"

Hadrian sniffed. "A harpy's nest is easy to find. You just follow your nose."

"That doesn't help much."

"Well, a map can help too." Hadrian fumbled in his apron pockets. "Ah, here it is." He pulled out a scroll and handed it to Driskoll.

A strange sensation came over Driskoll as he took the roll of parchment. It felt familiar. It was almost as if there was a note on the scroll that said *Open me. Read me.* When had he felt that before?

He unrolled it and looked at Hadrian. "It's a map of the ruins. Where did you get this?"

Hadrian waved him aside. "That's not important. What is important is that we get that dagger back from the harpies."

Driskoll looked at the map again. "So why would the harpies take the dagger?"

"Why do harpies do anything? They're thieving, murdering monsters. They're probably working for the beast."

"What beast?"

"The mantlehorn, boy! What other beast is there?"

"I heard them say something about a deal," Driskoll said. "I think they said something like 'deal off.'"

Hadrian waved his arms impatiently. "Just go to the ruins, boy. Get the dagger back. Before the beast gets it. Before it's too late."

Driskoll remembered the vision of Kellach and Willeona and the dagger dripping blood. Hadrian was right. He had to do something.

He looked up at the starry sky. It was still hours until dawn.

"But I'll never get past the Westgate," he moaned. "The watchers don't let anyone pass while it's still dark."

Hadrian grew more and more agitated. His entire body was shaking, and his wizened old face contorted. For a second,

Driskoll thought he saw a flash of silver streak across his wrinkled features. Driskoll blinked, and it was gone.

"Just use the map, boy." Hadrian said. "You're a scroll tender, aren't you?"

"Yeah, but what does that have to do with—"

"And your father is captain of the watch, is he not?"

"Yes, but—"

"Then go! The map will help you only for a few minutes." Hadrian pushed him along the path.

"But—"

"No buts, boy. Get moving." Hadrian gave one final heave, sending Driskoll almost halfway down the path. He turned, but Hadrian was hobbling back toward the castle. Driskoll stared at him for a moment. Hadrian had finally gone batty. How was Driskoll ever going to get through the Westgate?

Wait, he thought. Hadrian said to use the map. Maybe it would show him a secret passage out of the city.

He looked at the map in his hands, and he nearly jumped. His hands had grown larger in the last few seconds.

Oh no, he thought. Another cursed scroll.

But as he looked down, he realized that he was suddenly taller. The rest of his body had grown too. And he wasn't wearing his own clothes. The symbol of the city of Curston was stitched in gold thread across his chest, and a dark velvet cape swept around him. He was wearing a uniform.

The uniform of the captain of the watch.

CHAPTER

24

Driskoll put his palms to his broad chest and then to his muscular shoulders. Was it possible that he wasn't Driskoll anymore? He touched his cheek and felt the rough stubble of shaven whiskers.

Yes, it was true. He was Torin, the captain of the watch.

Driskoll grinned. The map would come in handy later on.

He took an unsteady step forward and fell in the dirt. He would have to get used to his new height, and fast. Hadrian had said the map would help him only for a few minutes.

Driskoll stood up and tried a few more steps. He was seeing everything from about two feet above his usual perspective, and it all seemed strangely smaller. But by the time he made it down the path, he was a little more comfortable in his taller body.

He walked through the city streets, trying to imitate his father's long, purposeful strides. He began to feel confident, like his father. Maybe the map was helping him with that, too.

But as he approached the Westgate, he faltered. What if the

watchers could tell he wasn't Torin? And worse yet, what if his dad was there, at the gate?

He looked at the towering, ironbound gate. Two huge watchers stood before it. One of them was Mobrick, the same watcher that Kellach had tried to intimidate the other night.

Driskoll wanted to run, but the watchers had already noticed him.

"Who goes there?"

Driskoll took a step forward, and the watchers snapped to attention. It was working. They thought he was Torin. Driskoll took a few more strides forward. He tried to look determined.

"What are your orders, sir?" Mobrick called.

Driskoll froze. He hadn't thought he would actually have to speak. What if his voice was his own?

"Sir?"

Driskoll stood staring at them. He didn't know what to do. The watchers were waiting. A few more seconds of silence from him and they would begin to wonder.

"Uh," a deep voice rumbled out of Driskoll's mouth.

"Yes, sir?"

The watchers looked at him expectantly. He took a deep breath.

"Open the gate," he said in a deep, somewhat shaky voice.

"But sir, it's not light yet. The rules, sir."

"Open the gate," Driskoll said again. It came out loud and clear.

Mobrick didn't move. He studied Driskoll for a moment.

"You do not need to remind me of the rules, " Driskoll said. "Now open the gate."

Mobrick squinted at Driskoll suspiciously until the other watcher nudged him. "Go," the watcher said. "The captain of the watch commands you to open the gate."

"Right, " Mobrick said, still looking at Driskoll. "The captain."

Driskoll glared at Mobrick. He wasn't sure, but he felt as though he was looking up at Mobrick, rather than down. But Mobrick finally looked away and signaled to the gatehouse. Instantly, a stream of watchers filed out and began to heave at the ironbound logs barring the gate.

It seemed to take forever, and Driskoll was suddenly aware of being closer to the ground. He glanced down quickly and saw his own worn and shabby boots beneath the dark blue captain's uniform.

Hurry, he thought as the watchers slowly drew back the last log and pushed at the huge gate.

Driskoll slipped through the opening, painfully aware that his head met the watchers' shoulders and that his uniform was dissolving into a patched blue jacket and a ragged shirt.

"Now close the gate," he called over his shoulder in a distinctly higher voice. He took a few steps forward and glanced back as the gate inched closed.

Mobrick was peering out the opening, a nasty grin on his face.

"Go to the ruins," he sneered. "And don't worry, little Knight. Your father will never know what became of you."

The gate thudded shut, and Mobrick was gone.

∎ ∎ ∎ ∎ ∎

It would be a few more hours until the sun rose, and Driskoll looked around the dark, lonely road. Who knew what kind of demons or monsters lay waiting along here?

This was their home after all, and Driskoll was an intruder. He was back to his own size again, but at least he had the map. It would help him find the harpy nest—as long as nothing else found him first.

A shiver ran down his spine as he unrolled the old map. The darkness made it hard to see, but something was wrong. The parchment was blank.

Driskoll turned it over. There was nothing on the other side either.

Driskoll studied the empty parchment. How could this be? He took a step forward, but he still wasn't used to his normal size and he tripped, landing hard on his ankle.

He cried out as the pain shot up his leg, "Dragon dung!"

Now what was he going to do? The map was no longer any help, he wasn't huge, brave Torin anymore, and his ankle felt sprained. He was helpless, exposed, and probably lost.

As he slowly heaved himself up, he came face to face with two tiny black eyes. They looked familiar. They were set on an oversized, green face.

The eyes looked up, and Driskoll followed them to another pair of black eyes, about ten feet above him. They were on a similar, though larger green face. Its ivory horns were blood-stained, and it looked at Driskoll with flat black eyes. The ogre mage towered above him, covered in armor and wielding a heavy sword about as long as Driskoll was tall.

Mommy had come.

Driskoll scrambled around, trying to move away. But his leg felt dead against him. The baby ogre pointed its stubby finger in Driskoll's face as it jumped and babbled at its mother.

In a single quick movement, the larger creature reached out and grabbed Driskoll with one arm. Driskoll struggled as it cradled him in its suffocating grip and dangled its sword like a baby rattle. It let out a howling, demonic laugh.

All this attention apparently wasn't what the little one had in mind for Driskoll. It stomped its feet and bellowed some more, mimicking what had happened the night before when it had chased the knife and grabbed it. It pretended to howl in pain just as it had done then.

"Tattletale," Driskoll muttered. But he felt a change in the way the ogre was holding him. It looked down at him, and its black teeth were bared. It stuffed him under its arm, its sharp armor pinching him. It began tramping back to the ruins.

Driskoll struggled with all of his might to break free while Junior stuck its thumb in its mouth and ran alongside them.

The ogre climbed the hill to the ruins, passed through the old city's crumbled gates, and ambled through the old streets. Finally the ogre mommy stopped before an ancient brick well. Since Driskoll was facing down, he could see that it dug far into the earth.

The ogre held him by his feet, dangling him over the well. So this was how it was all going to end, he thought. Everything— his plans to be a great bard, to be a heroic Knight of the Silver Dragon—it was all ending just because Junior had to go and tell Mommy about the big bully with the flaming knife.

Bump.

Driskoll felt something large slam into the ogre from behind. Its head jerked upward, and the impact sent Driskoll flying. Just as he was about to fall into the well, something large pinched his shoulder, and with a jerk, he began moving upward.

Something was carrying him, and whatever it was, it smelled bad. He looked down and could see the ogre mage dazedly looking for Driskoll. Junior jumped and pointed, but Driskoll kept moving up.

He heard a loud *caw* above him and looked up.

CHAPTER

25

Ruida had him in her talons, and she was flying away. He waved good-bye to Mommy Ogre and Junior, who were both howling on the ground below.

Ruida crowed loudly as she headed for a high cliff. She dropped him hard, and he landed face down in a pile of mud and bones and he wasn't sure what else.

"Other harpies not here, so house safe for now," Ruida said, perching on the side of the nest, with her horrible face twisted into a grimace. "But Bardman not stay. Harpies be back soon. Harpies not like men."

Driskoll tried to sit up, but between the throbbing pain in his ankle and the overpowering smell of the place the harpies called home, he fell back and threw up.

"Snacks," Ruida said softly, licking her foul lips.

Driskoll tried to ignore her as he dragged himself to another side of the nest.

"Ruida promise to repay Bardman," she crowed. "Save from ogre. But why Bardman come to ruins?"

Driskoll sat up queasily and rubbed his ankle. "I'm looking for the dagger. The Dagger of Doom. You took it from my brother."

Ruida shook her head. "Other harpies take it from Wizard-boy. Not Ruida. But harpies not have dagger anymore. Give back to Four Legs."

Driskoll groaned. He was too late.

"Four Legs say she give us good old meat for bringing dagger back."

"Wait, Four Legs is a she?" Driskoll put it together. A she with Four Legs. A girl with four legs. A deer has four legs. Four Legs is a mantlehorn. The mantlehorn is Willeona. So Willeona *was* wrapped up in all this! He knew it! But there was one thing that didn't make sense.

"I thought you said you stole the dagger from the mantle-horn, not for her?" he said.

"Eh?" Ruida looked at him. "Ha, ha. Ruida tell Bardman story, ha, ha."

"Okay. Just tell me the story."

She pushed her hand through her knotted black hair and began.

"Harpies supposed to get new house if they steal dagger from Four Legs. So harpies steal it. Easy. Only Four Legs shoot Ruida with arrow. Hurt real bad." Ruida stopped and looked at her wing. "She crash into tower and get stuck at Wizardman house."

"Okay, Driskoll said. "But what about the dagger?"

She grimaced. "So," she continued, "other harpies go to new house, but new house turn out to be castle. Harpies no

151

want castle. They want nest! Harpies say deal off. Other harpies go get dagger from Wizardboy. Then give dagger back to Four Legs."

"Deal off," Driskoll said. "That's what they were shouting today. Deal off. But who did you make the deal with? Who were you stealing the dagger for?"

"Don't know, Bardman. Other harpies do deals."

Driskoll could think of two people who would build a castle in return for a dagger. Hadrian and Scraper. Scraper had already tried to kill Oswald over the dagger scroll. And he had that tattoo on his hand. That proved it. He must have promised them a new house if the harpies got the dagger for him.

Driskoll remembered the way Scraper had looked at the dagger when Kellach was cutting rocks with it. He'd looked furious. Maybe he was jealous that Kellach had the dagger.

He had to get back to the castle. He could tell Hadrian. Hadrian would know what to do.

"Ruida," he said, "I've got to get to the castle in the city. You know, where you stayed in the moat. But I can't walk. I hurt my ankle. I know you can't take me past the watchers, but maybe you could get me to the castle."

"Yah, Bardman, we go now."

"Okay," he said. "Just give me a minute to rest. My ankle—"

"No Bardman," Ruida said, pointing at a noisy red cloud of harpies moving steadily toward them. "We go *now*."

Driskoll didn't have to argue. The flock of harpies was flying fast, and Ruida was old and injured. He had no idea how they were going to get away from them. Ruida grasped his shoulders, and her talons dug into his flesh. If this was how a harpy repaid you, Driskoll didn't want to do any more favors for them.

He heard the other harpies squawking close behind as Ruida swooped low to avoid them. They exchanged some curses that made Driskoll's hair stand on end.

The harpies backed off as they saw that she was headed toward the city.

"Ruida," he yelled up to her. "Why were they chasing you?"

"Harpies hate men," she croaked. "Ruida captured by Wizardman. Live in Wizardman's cage. Harpies want to kill Ruida for disgrace."

"They'd kill you just for that? I'm sure if Zendric had known, he would never have put you in the cage."

"It's okay, Bardman. Ruida old. Die soon anyway. Harpies know that. They stop chasing old Ruida."

They flew toward the city. It was an odd way to travel, hanging beneath a harpy. Driskoll's shoulders were now so numb with pain that he couldn't feel her sharp talons digging into his shoulders. His legs dangled beneath him, and he could see the Westgate ahead.

"The castle is on the other side of town. We can get over the wall on that side. There will be fewer watchers over there."

Ruida flew in a wide circle to avoid the gate, and Driskoll breathed a sigh of relief as they passed it without so much as a single arrow shot.

They were at the wall within minutes. Ruida had to gain some altitude to get up and over the wall. Driskoll could hear her labored breathing and hoped she could make it.

Two watchers patrolled the wall.

"We'll just have to try to get past them," Driskoll said. But no sooner had he spoken than one of the watchers happened to turn in their direction. Driskoll could see him pointing at them and pulling out his bow.

Ruida climbed higher, gasping for breath. He felt an arrow whir by his head.

"Ruida must leave Bardman here," she crowed. "Harpy way."

Driskoll felt his stomach drop as Ruida dipped into a dive.

"But won't the other harpies come and help you?" he asked.

"No, Bardman. I told you harpies mad at Ruida. Leave Ruida alone to die."

To die? Suddenly Driskoll realized what had just happened. Ruida had been hit with an arrow.

She wasn't diving. She was falling.

Driskoll looked below. Somehow Ruida had managed to make it far enough over the wall so that they were directly over the castle area.

She continued falling and Driskoll could see the tower just below. With one last shriek of pain, she spread her wings to break the fall. A few feet from the ground, she let go of Driskoll's shoulders and he landed in the grass just before she slammed into the earth.

He rushed across the clearing, where he found her slumped against a pile of rubble, not moving.

Driskoll reached out and shook the harpy gently. "Ruida? Are you okay?"

Ruida didn't answer.

Driskoll felt sick. Ruida was a foul, odious monster who could have killed him easily, except that he had told her a story once. And now she had saved his life. He wished he had some rotting meat for her.

At last, Ruida rustled her wings weakly. "Go," she said. "Harpy way."

Driskoll gasped and knelt beside her. "But you're hurt! I can't leave you."

"Go, Bardman. Go!"

Driskoll got up. "The harpies have got to come and help you. They've just got to. That's what families do for one another."

But Ruida's eyes were already shut. He stared at her for a moment.

And then someone screamed.

CHAPTER

26

Driskoll turned away from the harpy and looked up at the tower. The scream had come from up there.

He limped painfully across the open area and up the tower steps. He finally reached the top and saw that Hadrian's door was ajar. He peeked inside. The room was in its usual messy condition. More crazy contraptions hung from the ceiling, and stacks of books lined the floor. A few flickering candles dripped wax on the tables.

But he couldn't see anyone. He didn't hear anything either. Slowly, carefully, he stepped inside.

He looked around. The room was deathly silent.

Yet Driskoll had that familiar feeling that someone was watching him. Looking everywhere, he inched his way through the maze of tables. He had to take a detour around a stack of books, and that was when he saw her.

Willeona.

She was sitting—slumping, really—on the floor, leaning against a table leg and holding the Dagger of Doom. Its tip was dripping blood. It was the exact same vision Driskoll had seen in the Knight of Mirrors' shield.

Driskoll moved slightly to one side, and she raised her head painfully.

"He is a mirror," she gasped. "Do not try to use it on him."

Driskoll noticed that Willeona's face was whiter than usual and that the left shoulder of her robes was soaked in blood.

"Do not use it on him," she repeated. Then her head rolled forward, and the dagger fell from her hand.

Driskoll ran and quickly scooped up the dagger. As he knelt by her, he felt a surge of heat behind him.

He glanced around quickly. Hadrian stood gazing at him.

"Hadrian," he said. "I didn't hear you come in."

"Don't touch her," Hadrian whispered, moving closer. "She's a beast."

The heat was getting stronger. Driskoll looked around, thinking that maybe the Knight of Mirrors had entered the room. He looked back at Hadrian.

Hadrian's face had undergone an amazing change. He had always looked confused and glassy-eyed before, but now his eyes had a steely, almost angry, look to them. His white eyebrows pointed downward, and his thin lips were curled so that all Driskoll could see behind the white beard were brown teeth.

"So you made it back from the ruins, did you?" Hadrian said in a low voice. He didn't sound like Hadrian anymore either. He sounded much more confidant, and there was something else. Something familiar.

"I thought you would certainly be killed by the ogre mage," Hadrian said.

"How do you know about the ogre?"

"I know them well," he answered. "When the little one complained to me about you three, I thought it would be a perfect way to get rid of you. So I sent you there with one of my maps. I hope you liked my map."

"Liked it? It made me look like my father, but then it turned blank as soon as I left the city walls. What kind of map was that?" Driskoll realized that he didn't have the map any longer. He must have dropped it when the ogre picked him up.

Hadrian chuckled. "I am an inventor . . . and a wizard. And I have a certain talent for inventing magical documents. They can be very useful sometimes."

Driskoll didn't like the look in Hadrian's eyes, and he held the dagger tightly. "What do you mean 'magical documents'?"

"Ah," he said. "Like the one you are carrying in your pocket. The one you stole from the bard."

"I didn't steal it," Driskoll said. "I borrowed it. And how do you know—"

"I know a great many things," Hadrian interrupted. "All we need is your brother. He should be here shortly."

Driskoll gasped, "Where is he?"

Hadrian sighed. "He will be here soon, and you will kill each other over the dagger."

"No one's going to kill anybody," Driskoll blurted.

Hadrian shrugged. "You will find it much easier than you think. It was very easy to poison the old bard, for example."

"*You* poisoned him? I thought Scraper—"

"Well, yes, of course, he did."

Now Driskoll was really confused. "I don't understand—"

Hadrian sighed, and then his eyes flashed. "Well I don't remember much," he said in an exaggerated tone, as if he were someone else making fun of Hadrian. "But I suppose I can tell you a few things.

"When Scraper came to oversee the castle construction, he saw the drawing I had made of the dagger. He asked me about it, and I told him the truth. That it came from the ruins. I did not tell him that I had created it there. I have lived there for centuries, you see. And when I heard that the Knights of the Silver Dragon had returned to Curston, I was determined to find the dagger and use it to destroy the order. They do not deserve to go on. In the ruins, I met a group of harpies. In exchange for building them a new house, they promised to find the dagger and bring it to me."

Driskoll shook his head. How could Hadrian, the crazed old man be saying such things? He could hardly believe his ears. "But what does Scraper have to do with all this?"

Hadrian leered at the dagger for a moment and then continued in his new and powerful voice.

"Scraper has dwarf blood running through him, and the dwarves have searched for the Dagger of Doom too. They wish to destroy it. When he saw my drawing, he stole it and brought it to your friend, the bard, thinking that even drawings of the dagger are evil and should be erased. When I learned of his actions, I was beside myself with rage."

Hadrian shook as he spoke. "But then I found out that you, a new Knight, were working as a scroll tender for the old bard. And I realized what an opportunity that might be. Now that you knew of the dagger, you would begin to look for it too. Perhaps you might come here. And you did. I must say I am impressed with how quickly you found me. And you even brought your brother. It was more than I could ask for.

"Of course, I had to get rid of Oswald. He actually reads all those old scrolls, and he knew far too much about my past and the legend of the dagger. I knew it was a matter of time before he began telling everyone what he knew about me, so I had to get rid of him. And poisons are another of my great inventions . . .

"Of course, I cannot travel in the city," he added as if it were obvious. "I gave Scraper a disguise and told him to deliver the celestial mead to the bard for me. I convinced him it had to do with getting rid of the dagger. The fool believed me, and he had no idea that it was poisoned." Hadrian shook his head. "Considering what a mess he nearly made of things, it was only right that he take the blame for the poisoning."

Driskoll's mind spun with all of this new information. He looked at Willeona lying on the floor and looked up at the sound of footsteps coming up the stairs.

Kellach burst into the room.

Hadrian whipped around. "Boy," he cried, instantly returning to his old doddering self. "Help. I think he's killed her."

"What?" Driskoll shouted. "I didn't—"

Kellach ran to Willeona. His eyes went from Willeona, now lying in a pool of blood, to Driskoll.

"No, I didn't do this," Driskoll said. "She was like this when I came in here."

Driskoll held the dagger out to his older brother. "I swear, I didn't do it."

Kellach grabbed the dagger. "She didn't do anything to you," he said. "Why didn't you listen to me?"

Kellach's eyes were blazing.

"No, Kellach, I didn't do anything, I swear!"

Kellach pointed the dagger at Driskoll. "You never listen to me, do you? I told you—"

"Kellach, I didn't do this. You have to believe me!" Driskoll could see Hadrian doing a wild dance behind Kellach as the room grew hotter.

Kellach continued pointing the dagger at Driskoll.

Driskoll's skin prickled with heat as Kellach held the dagger over his own head, staring wildly at Driskoll and taking aim.

Driskoll pulled out his sword.

"I can't believe I'm doing this, Kellach," he shouted. But before he could move forward to strike, he felt something sharp against his chest. Kellach had been too fast for him. The tip of the dagger touched Driskoll's chest.

"You can't be serious, Kellach," Driskoll whispered. "You're not going to kill me." But Driskoll saw the look in Kellach's eyes. It was a wild sort of crazy anger he'd never seen before.

"I've never been more serious about anything in my life."

All Driskoll could do was close his eyes and wait for the dagger to strike.

CHAPTER

27

"L ook," Kellach shouted. "Look down."

Driskoll opened his eyes.

The dagger was still pointed at him. But instead of plunging it into his chest, Kellach was holding it steady. And in his other hand, he held a small pocket-sized mirror.

"I'm not trying to kill you," Kellach said. "You may have tried to kill me and Willeona and everyone else, but you're still my brother. I was just trying to show you this."

Driskoll looked at the dagger. He could see Kellach's name burned into the blade and the runes on the guard:

$$=V i 1 \ ? = \Pi W \Diamond$$

Kellach pointed at the dagger's shiny blade. "Look at it, Driskoll. The dagger is a mirror. Don't you get it? Mirrors reflect things. Mirrors make things look backward."

Kellach tipped the pocket-sized mirror so that it reflected the runes. In the mirror, they read in reverse:

Driskoll stared at the reflection.

"I'm the owner," Kellach said. "And while I've got the dagger, I'm protected. I will live."

Driskoll's knees felt weak. He wanted to sit down. "Oh, Kellach," he whispered. "I'm so sorry."

Hadrian stopped dancing. He turned and stared at them.

There was a choking sound coming from the floor. It was Willeona. She was struggling to get up. Driskoll and Kellach ran to her.

She reached for the wound on her shoulder and looked at Kellach.

"Do not aim it at him," she whispered. "I tried to kill him with the dagger. But he is a mirror too. Instead the dagger killed me—" She closed her eyes, and her head fell forward again.

Hadrian growled. "And now I shall kill them too!"

Suddenly Hadrian's arms stiffened at his sides. His entire body became like a statue. And something else was happening. His body was turning . . . silver. As if a silver armor was growing over it. Mirrored armor.

Driskoll's mouth dropped open as he realized what was happening. "Hadrian? You're the Knight of Mirrors?"

"Yes," the bone-chilling voice of the Knight of Mirrors came out of the visor. "I used my magic to build the greatest armor the world has ever known," the knight said. "A mirror."

He held up the shield, and they could see a vision of Driskoll holding the dagger, just as he had been holding it while he bent over Willeona.

"Is this what you saw in your room last night?" There was a hint of mocking laughter in the knight's voice now. "When you thought your own brother was trying to kill you."

Kellach nodded. "So it was you. That's why it felt so hot just before it happened."

"And now," the knight moved toward them, "you must want to kill me. After all I have done. Go ahead, use the dagger."

Kellach raised the dagger and aimed at the knight.

Driskoll turned. "Wait, Kellach. Willeona said he's a mirror. Remember your spell the other night that sent us to the ruins."

Kellach nodded, and Driskoll knew that Kellach had worked that out, too. His spell had backfired the other night because the Knight of Mirrors was a ghost with a magical, mirrored armor. It reversed everything, including spells.

Driskoll pulled on Kellach's arm. "Don't do it! If you throw the dagger at Hadrian, it will come back and kill you. It's what he wants."

Driskoll looked up at the ghostly knight. "It's been you all along, hasn't it? Every time we have an argument, you're there. You've been pushing us to fight ever since we came here. You're the reason we keep arguing. You made me draw my sword. Because you know that the dagger comes to brothers who can't get along. You want us to kill each other. But why?"

The knight towered over them. His armor shone brilliantly. "The dagger tears brothers apart," he said.

Kellach held the dagger up in the candlelight. "Yes, just like it tore you and your brother apart. You hate us because we're Knights of the Silver Dragon. Knights and brothers. You want us to die. Our anger is what keeps you going, isn't it? Every time we argue, you get stronger, don't you?"

Driskoll looked at his brother and then back at the knight. "Well, guess what? No one will be killed tonight. Right, Kellach?" Kellach nodded.

An explosive roaring came from the knight as he shook with rage. "If you won't kill each other, I will have to do it myself!"

Before Kellach and Driskoll had time to move away, he thrust the mirrored shield in their faces.

Driskoll heard a *clang* as the Dagger of Doom fell to the ground.

He struggled to reach for it, but something was forcing him to look into the vision in the shield. He could see himself and Kellach. But it wasn't a vision. It was a reflection in a mirror.

Then there was a blinding flash of lightning, and it felt as if the shield was opening up.

Slam! Driskoll fell into a glass door, knocking his head and nearly passing out from the pain. He tried to turn, but something was blocking him in the front and in the back. It was the glass door, and it had closed in on him from all sides, flattening him inside it.

"Kellach? Kellach!"

"I'm right here." Kellach's voice came from next to him.

"We're trapped!" Driskoll shouted. "We're inside something."

"Yeah," Kellach said. "I think we're actually in the shield."

"Yes," the Knight answered from somewhere behind them. "And now that I have the dagger, you will remain inside of it forever. You cannot escape."

165

He was right. Driskoll could not move one inch of his body. He felt as if he were in a flat glass coffin. He was breathing hard.

Kellach's voice came from beside him. "I don't think there's very much air in here. Take shallow breaths."

But Driskoll was already having trouble breathing.

The Knight leaned the shield containing the two boys against the wall. He walked around and stood in front of it.

"And now, this is the hour when the Knight of Mirrors shall deliver brothers to their doom. I shall again destroy this castle. And all who live and work here."

From inside the glass, Driskoll could see the tools falling from the wall. The room shook like an earthquake.

"See," the knight said as books and inventions toppled all around him, "my anger destroys the castle. As it destroys you."

Rocks and pebbles were sliding down the walls. Driskoll took shallow breaths, but he didn't see how he could hold on much longer. He couldn't tell if Kellach was still breathing.

A lit candle fell off a table. The flames began to crawl across the room, toward Willeona, who lay unconscious on the floor.

"How did he do all this?" Driskoll whispered.

"It must be some kind of spell."

Driskoll was relieved to hear Kellach's voice. He was still breathing, still alive. Driskoll felt light-headed, but at the word "spell," a memory tickled at the corner of his thoughts.

The flames were darting around the room as the Knight danced. Driskoll couldn't think. He wanted to close his eyes. What had Kellach just said? Oh yes, a spell. And then he remembered.

"Kellach!" he whispered. "Curse me!"

"What?" Kellach's voice came out thick and sleepy sounding.

"A curse. No, not a curse. What's it called? A . . . a spell. What was that thing again? The Silencing Spell? But the castle messed it up . . ."

The room was crumbling around them. It shook harder, and they felt the shield being tossed around.

"Remember, Kellach?"

"Yeah, you were . . . you were shrieking."

"Right. Shrieking. So come on, Kellach. Curse me!"

Kellach was dangerously silent for a moment.

"Kellach!"

"Right." Kellach spoke the words slowly and thickly. He hoped Kellach was saying it clearly enough. He hoped the castle magic would mess it up, just like before.

Kellach finished muttering. Nothing happened for a moment.

The room was a blur of gray as everything fell around them. More small fires had started. Driskoll opened his mouth. Nothing came out.

Oh no. The curse hadn't worked.

He could see Willeona lying on the floor and the flames inching closer to her. He opened his mouth once more and yelled. He heard something like a tiny shriek. It wasn't enough to break open the glass. He heard another shriek too. Kellach.

The air inside the shield was growing thinner. Driskoll was so dizzy he felt like he was about to pass out. But he opened his mouth one final time and yelled at the top of his lungs.

There was a great roaring, a shattering of glass.

They were on the floor.

The knight was still dancing madly around the flames. Driskoll took a deep breath and yelled again. He heard Kellach next to him screaming with all his might, and he was never happier to hear his brother yelling.

The knight turned to them slowly.

A small crack erupted in the armor, running down the center. Suddenly, the armor shattered, sending small pieces everywhere, and the knight fell to the floor. The visor of his helmet opened, and a puff of red smoke burst out and flew out of the slit window.

Inside, the helmet was empty. The Knight of Mirrors was no more.

CHAPTER

28

Kellach ran across the room to Willeona as the flames licked his feet.

Kellach reached through the fire and grasped hold of her arms. "Help me carry her," he yelled over the roar of the flames.

Together they lifted her and carried her down the circular stairway.

But it was too late. The steps were collapsing right in front of them. "We'll have to make a jump for it," Kellach yelled in his high-pitched voice. "Hold on."

Suddenly Driskoll felt himself being lifted off the ground, still holding Willeona. The three of them flew down the chasm that used to be the steps.

They shot out the open doorway, propelled by Kellach and the force of the exploding tower.

They landed in the grass near the little chapel and watched as the white tower crumbled to the ground.

Driskoll lay on the grass, panting and wheezing. His ankle

was throbbing, and he saw that Kellach's hands had been burned by the flames.

Kellach leaned over and shook Willeona by the shoulder. "Are you all right?" he shrieked.

Willeona slowly opened her eyes. She smiled and put her hand on his shoulder. "Do not worry about me," she said weakly. "Mantlehorn are half celestial. Already I feel the healing begin." She leaned up on her elbows.

"I'm so sorry, Willeona," Driskoll said, after his voice had returned to normal again. "This was all my fault. I thought you were to blame for all this. But it was Hadrien all along."

"Hush." She hesitated and clutched her shoulder. "If this is anyone's fault, it is mine. You see, the dagger was made by my people. I gave it to Cor many years ago, and it nearly killed him."

"Nearly killed him?" Driskoll asked. "But the legend said the dagger did kill him."

Willeona shook her head. "The legend is wrong."

"What do you mean?"

Willeona sat back with a sigh. "Cor was a Knight of the Silver Dragon. He saved my people from our enemies many times, and he became one of my closest friends. And as a reward for protecting me and my people so valiantly, I gave Cor the dagger. The dagger is powerful. It is able to cut through almost any material, including stone. I knew Cor's brother, Adrian, would be jealous of the dagger. He was a mason. He would covet the dagger's properties, and he had long harbored bitter feelings toward his brother. So I secretly forged the 'Owner Live' runes into it as a protection and magically inscribed Cor's name into the blade.

While Cor's name marked the dagger, he couldn't be killed by a sword or dagger of any kind."

Driskoll looked at his brother. "So that's why Kellach didn't die when the knight came into our room and attacked him with it. He was protected because his name was on the blade."

Kellach nodded. "But Cor didn't know what the runes meant. And he felt sorry for his brother and tried to give the dagger to him—"

Driskoll interrupted, "Wait a second, Kellach. You knew the real legend all along?"

"Willeona told me the true story after I accused you of trying to kill me." Kellach shrugged. "I would have told you, but we couldn't find you."

Driskoll rubbed his sore ankle and thought of Ruida. "It's a long story." He turned back to Willeona. "So what happened after you gave Cor the dagger?"

Willeona continued, "As I expected, Adrian was jealous of his brother's reputation as a Knight and of my gift. He fought bitterly with Cor that night, and plunged the dagger into Cor's chest. Thinking his brother had been killed, Adrian fled Promise Castle in shame, and the castle fell into ruins. But as time went on, instead of accepting responsibility for his rage, he blamed the Knights of the Silver Dragon for his crime. He vowed to reclaim the dagger and seek vengeance against the Knights." Willeona shook her head slowly. "And he continued to do so, even after death claimed his body and his spirit roamed the land."

Driskoll felt a shiver run down his spine. "So Hadrian was Adrian's ghost?"

Willeona frowned. "You could say that. As Adrian lay dying,

172

he used his powers as a wizard to ensure he would live to see his vengeance enacted. To do so, he cast a spell that would allow him to live part of the time in his mortal form. And when his anger took over, he transformed into his spirit form, the Knight of Mirrors."

Willeona fingered the glass locket around her neck, and her eyes darkened. "In my anger I took this from Adrian after he tried to kill Cor. And I have kept it ever since as a reminder that I am bound to guard the dagger owner."

Slowly, Willeona removed the locket and tossed it into the rubble. "I think it is no longer needed," she said, smiling.

Driskoll looked at Willeona. "Whatever happened to Cor?"

"Because of the runes on the dagger, Cor didn't die. But still, I feared for his life. I took Cor and the dagger back to our mountain to protect him from his brother. Cor lived out his days with my people. He was a hero to us all. After his death, the dagger passed down through generations of my people. We have waited many years for a new name to appear on the dagger.

"You wondered why the dagger has Kellach's name on it," she said, turning to face Driskoll. "But after today, you should wonder no longer. The dagger is destined for a Knight of the Silver Dragon who proves himself worthy.

"When Kellach's name appeared on the blade, I left my mountain to deliver it to him. But Adrian was watching, and he was determined to reclaim the dagger. He did not understand that the dagger would never be truly his. It has a destiny all its own. He convinced the harpies to steal it from me. And then he tried to use it to kill Kellach that first day you were here on the castle grounds."

Driskoll gasped. "So it was Hadrien who threw the knife at Kellach."

Willeona nodded. "I had come to the castle, hoping to retrieve the dagger. And I was watching everything. I might have let Kellach keep the dagger that day, but I knew he wasn't ready for it. He did not understand its powers. I took the dagger and gave it to him later after I could explain the meaning of the gift."

Kellach looked down, examining his burned hands. "But I nearly squandered it by giving it to Hadrian. I was so angry at you, Driskoll. How stupid!" He shook his head.

Willeona patted his shoulder. "Thank the gods that the magnificent nest Hadrian promised the harpies never came to fruition. They were angry and they stole the dagger back, returning it to me. I explained the real story behind the legend to Kellach. Then I came here to stop this dangerous vengeful game that I had begun so many years ago with my gift. But I did not fully realize the power of the Knight of Mirrors."

Driskoll nodded. "Everything you do to him reflects back on you."

She nodded and crawled to her feet. "You were one of the few to see through the Knight of Mirrors' powers. You saw that his rage was his weapon, but it was also his downfall. Without you, Driskoll, all would have been lost."

Embarrassed, Driskoll looked away. He blinked in the early morning light at a moving shape carrying a torch. Someone was approaching.

It was Scraper.

He knelt next to them. "The Dagger of Doom has destroyed the tower," he said in a hushed voice.

"It wasn't the dagger," Kellach said. "It was a ghost pretending to be a knight."

Scraper pulled a striped leaf out of his bag and laid it on Willeona's shoulder. She looked up at him appreciatively, and he smiled at her. He put two more on Kellach's scorched hands.

"Be assured that the Dagger of Doom is at the heart of this destruction," Scraper said, turning away to look at the rubble. "It is a most evil weapon."

"The dagger isn't evil," Driskoll said quietly, rubbing his ankle. "It doesn't say 'evil' on it."

"Are you hurt?" Scraper asked, pulling another striped leaf out of his bag.

"Uh, I'm fine . . . ," Driskoll began, remembering how Scraper had delivered the poison to Oswald.

"Trust me," Scraper smiled. "It's ancient dwarf medicine. Not poison."

He wrapped the striped leaf around Driskoll's ankle. "I'm sorry if I frightened you in the city the other day," he said. "I was only trying to protect my people."

"By trying to strangle an innocent kid like me?"

Scraper smirked. "We dwarves have only to touch a stone structure and we know everything about it. And we can tell when a stone has been cut by magical means. The dagger has been known to our people as a dangerous, magical stonecutting tool. I, being half dwarf and half human, for some reason am particularly sensitive to the dagger. I can sense its presence ten feet away, and I sensed it on you. I knew that somehow you had the drawing still in your pocket.

"It has been my life's work to find and destroy that dagger.

I thought that because you had the drawing, that you were evil too. Now I know I was wrong about you. I trusted the wrong person."

"But Hadrian is gone now," Kellach said, kicking a small pebble toward the wall. Instead of magically sailing back, the stone fell straight down. "And the magic in these walls is gone too."

"You still have the drawing, do you not?" Scraper asked.

Driskoll nodded.

"You must destroy it," he said. "Take it to your bard master and place it in the cauldron."

"All right," Driskoll said. "But can it wait? I feel really sleepy right now."

Scraper smiled a little. "Aye, that would be the medicine taking effect. It might put you to sleep for a little while. All of you." Then he looked serious again. "I may know a lot about dwarf medicine, but I was not aware that the mead I gave to your bard master was poisoned," he said. "Had I known—"

"I'm sure Oswald will be okay," Driskoll reassured him.

"Yes." Scraper looked worried. "But he could have died. I have just come from there, in fact. He asked me to pass on a message to you."

"He did?"

"Yes, he asks that you be there a half hour earlier today, for you have much work to do, and he wants you to bring him some more chocolate."

Driskoll laughed. "Well then, you definitely don't have to worry about Oswald. He sounds just fine."

CHAPTER

29

Something smelled awful.

Driskoll rolled over onto his side and looked around the open area. The sun had risen fully on the castle ruins. And an ugly red woman perched on a boulder, grinning maniacally at him.

"Ruida!" He scrambled to sit up. "You're alive. Er, how long have you been sitting there?"

"Bardman sleep long time," Ruida croaked.

"I thought you were—"

"Yah, me too, Bardman. Dunno how I stay alive, but I do." She looked around. "Big mess around here."

"Yeah." He looked down at a sleeping Kellach. "So where will you go, Ruida?"

"Dunno," she said. "Can't go back to nest. Don't like Wizardman cage."

"Why don't you stay here? In the moat? I don't think anyone will be coming up here for a long time, so no one will bother you."

"That good idea, Bardman. Ruida like moat. Smell good. One problem, though. Ruida hurt again. Can't get food."

"I'll bring you food until your wing gets better."

"Good Bardman. Now wake up lazy Wizardboy."

She spread her wings and lifted off the ground, heading for the trapdoor. "CAWWWW!"

Kellach sat bolt upright. "What was that?"

Driskoll grinned. "A very old friend."

"How long have we been asleep?" Kellach yawned.

"Not long. The sun had risen when Scraper finally left."

"I wonder if he'll ever come back," Kellach mused.

"I don't know," Driskoll said. "Someone's always building something in Curston. I kind of hope he does. I liked cutting stone."

They were silent for a while as they looked around the open area.

"Kellach, Willeona will be okay, right?"

"Yeah. She's already gone back to her mountain. She's a half celestial, you know. That's about as close as you can get to being immortal. Unless you're a ghost."

"Kellach, I'm really sorry about everything I said about her."

"That's okay, Dris. I would probably have come to the same conclusion if you'd been acting like an idiot the way I was."

Kellach stood up and wandered to what was left of the tower.

"What are you looking for?" Driskoll asked, following close behind him.

"Hmm? Oh, well, I was thinking about what Willeona said

earlier. Remember? How the dagger chooses its own destiny?"

"Yeah."

Kellach lifted a rock away and peered under it. "The dagger selects someone worthy and then the name appears on the blade," he said. "But that person must prove himself a true Knight of the Silver Dragon to become the true owner. Willeona waited years for someone to carry on Cor's legacy. In fact," he continued, reaching deep into the rubble, "in its time the dagger has only had three owners."

"What do you mean three?" Driskoll looked at him. "I thought you and Cor were the only Knights who were worthy of bearing the dagger?"

Kellach drew something out from between the rocks. It looked like a long, narrow mirror.

"Cor, me, and . . ." He turned the mirror over and looked at it. Instantly Driskoll knew what it was. "I thought so," Kellach said, holding up the Dagger of Doom.

Driskoll looked at the blade. There was Kellach's name, as always. But another name had been burned in, right next to Kellach's: DRISKOLL.

Acknowledgments

Grateful acknowledgement to Nina Hess,
Jennifer DeChiara, and Marlene Perez

KNIGHTS
OF THE
SILVER
DRAGON
™

EXPLORE THE MYSTERIES OF CURSTON WITH KELLACH, DRISKOLL AND MOYRA

THE SILVER SPELL

Kellach and Driskoll's mother, missing for five years, miraculously comes home. Is it a dream come true? Or is it a nightmare?

KEY TO THE GRIFFON'S LAIR

Will the Knights unlock the hidden crypt before Curston crumbles?

CURSE OF THE LOST GROVE

The Knights spend a night at the Lost Grove Inn. Can they discover the truth behind the inn's curse before it discovers them?

Ask for KNIGHTS OF THE SILVER DRAGON books at your favorite bookstore!

For ages eight to twelve

For more information visit www.mirrorstonebooks.com

MORE ADVENTURES
FOR THE

FIGURE IN THE FROST

A cold snap hits Curston and a mysterious stranger holds the key to
the town's survival. But first he wants something...from Moyra. Will
Moyra sacrifice her secret to save the town?

DAGGER OF DOOM

When Kellach discovers a dagger of doom with his own name burned
in the blade, it seems certain someone wants him dead. But who?

THE HIDDEN DRAGON

The Knights must find the silver dragon who gave their order its name.
Can they make it to the dragon's lair alive?

**Ask for KNIGHTS OF THE SILVER DRAGON books
at your favorite bookstore!**

For ages eight to twelve

For more information visit www.mirrorstonebooks.com

THE NEW ADVENTURES

THE DRAGON QUARTET
The companions continue their quest to save Nearra.

DRAGON SWORD
Ree Soesbee

It's a race against time as the companions seek to prevent
Asvoria from reclaiming her most treacherous weapon.

DRAGON DAY
Stan Brown

As Dragon Day draws near, Catriona and Sindri stand as
enemies, on opposing sides of a feud between the most
powerful wizards and clerics in Solamnia.

DRAGON KNIGHT
Dan Willis

With old friends and new allies by his side, Davyn must
enlist the help of the dreaded Dragon Knight.

DRAGON SPELL
Jeff Sampson

The companions reunite in their final battle with
Asvoria to reclaim Nearra's soul.

Ask for Dragonlance: the New Adventures books at your favorite bookstore!
For ages ten and up.
For more information visit www.mirrorstonebooks.com